Please return / renew by date shown.

cops and mean ... renew it at ... Izzo was a marvelous food wri-
ter in addition to being a poet of violence and regret. His
books are filled with winning descriptions of Provençal meals
run through with the flavors of north Africa, Italy, Greece."
—Sam Sifton, *The New York Times*

"Caught between pride and crime, racism and fraternity,
tragedy and light, messy urbanization and generous beauty,
the city is for Jean-Claude Izzo a Utopia, an ultimate port of
call for exiles. There Montale, like Mr. Izzo himself perhaps,
is torn between fatalism and revolt, despair and sensual-
ism."—*The Economist*

"What makes Izzo's work haunting is his extraordinary abi-
lity to convey the tastes and smells of Marseilles, and the
way memory and obligation dog every step his hero
takes."—*The New Yorker*

"In Izzo's books . . . Marseilles is a '*ville selon nos coeurs,*' a city
in tune with our hearts, as we can read in the penultimate sentence of *Total Chaos*. A cosmopolitan, maritime city, greedy,
sensual and warm, but undermined by racism, hatred, money,
mafia, and religious fundamentalism—and passive complicity
in the face of these scourges."—Michel Samson, *Slow Food*

"Jean-Claude Izzo's Marseille trilogy . . . delve deep into the
guts of multiracial Marseilles, a city that is at once a hopeful
symbol of the Mediterranean's rich cultural past and an urban
dystopia burdened by unemployment, racism and violence . . .
Noir at its finest: compelling, sophisticated literature with a
biting social edge."—Hirsh Sawhney, *The Times Literary
Supplement*

"Like all tragic noir heroes, Montale treads a dangerously narrow line between triumphant savior and doomed avenger."—*The Village Voice*

"*Total Chaos* is undeniably literature . . . Part of this is due to Izzo's amazing characterization . . . Izzo takes a convention of noir—the lost soul who finds himself in vengeance—and packs it with enough realism to make it utterly lifelike . . . *Total Chaos* is a noir through and through, but it feels so real that it reminds us that the clichés of noir were originally drawn from real life."—*The Quarterly Conversation*

"A few years ago I was planning a trip to Madrid and Paris from Los Angeles. I was also deep into Jean-Claude Izzo's *Total Chaos* . . . By the time I finished the book, I had replaced the Paris leg of my trip with Marseilles. I'd found Lagavulin, the main character's scotch of choice. (Mine was always Laphroaig.) And a whole lot of interesting jazz . . . The story had leapt out from the book and into my life."—Valla Vakili, CEO, Small Demons

"Like the best American practitioners in the genre, Izzo refrains from any sugarcoating of the city he depicts or the broken and imperfect men and women who people it."—*Publishers Weekly*

"Jean-Claude Izzo's *Total Chaos* is a marvelous noir novel in which passions and feelings are thrown into the narrative mix without reserve and without gratuitousness."—*La Repubblica*

"*Total Chaos* . . . draws from the deep, dark well of noir . . . Izzo's plot is labyrinthine, but his novel is rich, ambitious and passionate, and his sad, loving portrait of his native city is amazing."—*The Washington Post*

SOLEA

ALSO BY

JEAN-CLAUDE IZZO

Total Chaos
Chourmo
A Sun for the Dying
The Lost Sailors
Living Tires

Jean-Claude Izzo

S O L E A

Translated from the French
by Howard Curtis

Europa
editions

Europa Editions
214 West 29th Street
New York, N.Y. 10001
www.europaeditions.com
info@europaeditions.com

This book is a work of fiction. Any references to historical events,
real people, or real locales are used fictitiously.

Copyright © 1998 and 2002 by Éditions Gallimard, Paris
First Publication 2007 by Europa Editions
Fourth printing, 2013

Translation by Howard Curtis
Original Title: *Solea*
Translation copyright © 2007 by Europa Editions
Eulogy for Jean-Claude Izzo © 2006 by Massimo Carlotto,
translation from the Italian by Michael Reynolds

All rights reserved, including the right of reproduction
in whole or in part in any form

This work has been published thanks to support from
the French Ministry of Culture – Centre National du Livre
Ouvrage publié avec le concours du Ministère
Français chargé de la Culture – Centre National du Livre

Library of Congress Cataloging in Publication Data is available
ISBN 978-1-60945-128-8

Izzo, Jean-Claude
Solea

Book design by Emanuele Ragnisco
www.mekkanografici.com

Printed in the USA

CONTENTS

EULOGY FOR JEAN-CLAUDE IZZO
by Massimo Carlotto

Recalling the work and the person of Jean-Claude Izzo will forever remain painful for those who knew him. Izzo was first and foremost a good person. It was impossible not to feel warmth for that slight man who always had an attentive, curious look in his eyes and a cigarette in his mouth. I met him in 1995, in Chambery, during the Festival du Premier Roman. Izzo was there to present *Total Chaos* (*Total Khéops*). I bought the book because its author stirred my interest: he seemed a little detached in many of those cultural gatherings, as if faintly annoyed by them, as he was most certainly annoyed by the quality of food and wine offered by the organizers. I read his book traveling between Chambery and Turin, where the Salone del Libro was underway. I found it a superb, innovative book, an exemplar in a genre that was finally starting to establish itself here in Italy. I recommended it to my publishers. And not long after Izzo arrived in Italy. A few sporadic meetings later, I went to Marseilles for a conference. Izzo was not there. He was in hospital. Everyone knew how serious his illness was. Marseilles was rooting for its noirist. Every bookshop in town filled its display windows with Izzo's books. Then, on January 26, Jean-Claude left us. He wasn't even fifty-five. He left us with many fond memories and several extraordinary novels that convincingly delineated the current now known as "Mediterranean Noir."

Autodidact, son of immigrant parents, his father a barman from Naples, his mother a Spanish seamstress. After lengthy battles as a left-wing journalist, having already written for film and television, and author of numerous essays, Izzo decided to take a stab at noir, penning his Marseilles Trilogy, *Total Chaos*, *Chourmo* and *Solea*. The protagonist: Fabio Montale; a cop.

Montale, son of immigrant parents, like Izzo, and child of the interethnic mix that is Marseilles, defiantly stakes out his ground in the city that gave birth to the *Front National*.[1] In *Solea*, Izzo writes:

It was good to be in Hassan's bar. There were no barriers of age, sex, skin color, or class among the regulars. We were all friends. Whoever came there to drink a *pastis* sure as hell didn't vote for the *Front National*. And they never had, not once, not like some others I knew. Here, in this bar, every single one of us knew why we were from Marseilles and not some other place, why we lived in Marseilles and not some other place. Friendship mixed with the smell of anise and filled the place. We communicated our feelings for one another with a single look. A look that took in our fathers' exile. It was reassuring. We had nothing to lose. We had already lost everything.

Izzo's writing is political, in the tradition of the French neo-polar novels[2], and the writing of Jean-Patrick Manchette. But compared with Manchette, who does not believe in direct political action inasmuch as he believes it is ineffective and doomed to failure, and who limits himself to using noir as an instrument with which to read reality, Izzo goes further. His

---

[1] The party was founded in 1972 by Jean-Marie Le Pen and is currently led by Marine Le Pen. It is generally considered to be of the far right, although its leaders deny this qualification.

[2] Neo-polar: the 1970s-80s version of the French mystery novel, after the rebirth of the genre following May '68. Often a politically-oriented novel with a social message.

use of the noir genre is not limited simply to description but penetrates deep into the heart of the incongruities, leaving room for sociological reflection and for a return to his generation's collective memory, and above all, gives sense to the present day. Via Montale's inner journey, Izzo declares his inexorable faith in the possibility of transformation, both individual and collective. The point that matters most to Izzo, politically speaking, that is, the point that cannot be abandoned, is the existence of a united culture. From the defeats of yesterday come the losers of today. From this perspective, Montale is an extraordinary figure. Son of marginalization, he joins the police so as to avoid the criminal margins. He abandons his group of childhood friends, a group that embodies multiple ethnic differences, but he will never forget his roots. This becomes a source for his feelings of guilt when faced with his role as cop in a society that is becoming increasingly intolerant. An internal gestation and growth obligates him to leave the police force and to become a loner in search of the justice that is not furnished by the courts. What gets him into trouble is the ethic of solidarity and the desire, common to culturally and ethnically mixed milieus, to find a place and a moment in which he can live peacefully.

On Mediterranean Noir

Solea, the concluding installment in Izzo's Marseilles Trilogy, is flamenco music's backbone, but also a song by Miles Davis. Indeed, music is one of the author's passions. Particularly jazz and the mix of Mediterranean rhythms that characterize contemporary southern European and North African music. In Izzo's writing, however, music does not simply represent rhythm and a source of nostalgia, but also a key to understanding generational differences. Montale contemplates the merits of rap music. He doesn't like it much, but his reflections represent a kind of understanding as to its intrinsic worth:

> I was floored by what it said. The rightness of the intentions behind it. The quality of the lyrics. They sang incessantly about the their friends' lives, whether at home or at the reform school.

With *Solea*, Jean-Claude Izzo gives substance to the political intuition that is the cornerstone of Mediterranean Noir. He understands that the sticking point the movement must face consists in the epochal revolutions that have transformed criminality. Babette Bellini's investigation[1] does not result in the typical affirmation of the Mafia's superiority and organized crime's collusion with higher powers. Izzo defines the outlines of Mediterranean Noir when he introduces into his novel the principal contradiction present in the crime-society dyad: the annual income of transnational criminal organizations worldwide is US$10,000 billion, a sum equal to the GDP of many single developing countries. The need to launder this mountain of dirty money is at the root of the dizzying increase in the corruption of institutions, of police forces. It is also the catalyst for strategic alliances between entrepreneurs, financial policing bodies, politics, and organized crime. The society in which we live is criminal inasmuch as it produces crime and "anti-crime," resulting in an endless spiral in which legal and illegal economies merge in a single model. Call it, if you will, a socio-economic "locomotive," as in the case of northeast Italy.

Mediterranean Noir, in this sense, departs from the existing conception of French Noir, and likewise from the

[1] Babette Bellini: a character in the Marseilles Trilogy. Journalist and activist, friend of Fabio Montale.

modern police novel. The novel no longer recounts a single "noir" story in a given place at a given moment but begins with a precise analysis of organized crime.

Another of Izzo's intuitions was his having individuated the Mediterranean as the geographical centre of the universal criminal revolution. There is a rich fabric of alliances in this region between new illegal cultures emerging from the east and from Africa. These alliances are influenced by local realities, which they in turn absorb into themselves. As a result, they possess the means to pursue direct negotiations with established power structures.

This is what Mediterranean Noir means: to tell stories with a wide swath; to recount great transformations; to denounce but at the same time to propose the culture of solidarity as an alternative.

For Thomas,
when he's big

It needs to be said one more time. This is a novel. Nothing of what you are about to read actually happened. But as I can't ignore what I read every day in the newspapers, it's inevitable that my story draws on real life. Because that's where everything is being decided—in real life. And in real life, the horror is greater—far greater—than anything that can possibly be invented. As for Marseilles, my city, always halfway between tragedy and light, it naturally reflects the threat hanging over us.

But something told me it was normal,
that there are certain moments in your life
when you have to do that—kiss corpses.

PATRICIA MELO

OUT OF SIGHT, NOT OUT OF MIND, MARSEILLES FOREVER

Her life was there, in Marseilles. There, beyond the mountains flaming red in this evening's sunset. It'll be windy tomorrow, Babette thought.

In the two weeks she'd spent in this village in the Cévennes, Le Castellas, she'd climbed up onto the ridge at the end of every day. Along the same path where Bruno led his goats.

The morning she'd arrived, she'd thought, Nothing changes here. Everything dies and is reborn. Even if there are more villages dying than being reborn. At some point, a man reinvents the old actions. And everything starts over. The overgrown paths again have a reason to exist.

"It's because the mountain remembers," Bruno had said, serving her a big bowl of black coffee.

She'd met Bruno in 1988. The first big assignment the newspaper had given her. Twenty years after May 1968, what had become of the militants?

As a young philosopher and anarchist, Bruno had fought on the barricades in Paris. *Run, comrade, the old world is after you.* That had been his only slogan. He'd run, throwing paving stones and Molotov cocktails at the riot police. He'd run with the tear gas exploding around him and the riot police at his heels. He'd run everywhere, through May and June, trying to keep one step ahead of the old world's happiness, the old world's dreams, the old world's morality. The old world's stupidity and corruption.

When the unions signed the Grenelle accords, and the workers went back to their factories and the students back to their faculties, Bruno realized he hadn't run fast enough. Nor had anyone in his generation. The old world had caught up with them. Money was the only dream now, the only morality. The only happiness left in life. The old world was making a new era for itself, an era of human misery.

That was how Bruno had told it to Babette. He talks like Rimbaud, she had thought, touched by his words, and attracted to this handsome forty-year-old man.

He and many others had left Paris. Heading for Ariège, the Ardèche, the Cévennes. Looking for abandoned villages. *Lo Païs*, they liked to call it. Another kind of revolution was emerging from the ruins of their illusions. A revolution based on nature and brotherhood. A sense of community. They were inventing a new country for themselves. A wilder, untamed France. Many left again after one or two years. Others persevered for five or six years. Bruno had stayed in this village he had revived. Alone, with his flock of goats.

That night, after the interview, Babette had slept with Bruno.

He'd asked her to stay.

But she couldn't. This wasn't her life.

Over the years, she had often been back to see him. Every time she was in or near the area. Bruno had a partner now, two children, electricity, a TV set and a computer, and he produced goat's cheese and honey.

"If you're ever in any trouble," he'd said to Babette, "come here. Don't hesitate. From up here all the way down to the valley, everyone's a friend of mine."

This evening, she was missing Marseilles a lot. But she didn't know when she could go back. Or even if she could go back. If she did, nothing, absolutely nothing could ever be the same. She wasn't just in trouble, it was worse than that. The horror of it was in her head all the time. As soon as she closed her eyes, she saw Gianni's corpse. And behind his corpse, those of Francesco and Beppe, which she hadn't seen but could imagine. Tortured, mutilated bodies. Surrounded by pools of black, congealed blood. Other corpses, too. Behind her. But mostly ahead of her. That was inevitable.

When she'd left Rome, frantic, scared to death, she hadn't known where to go. She needed somewhere safe. She needed to think it all through, as calmly as she could. To sort through her papers, put them in order, classify the information, check it all. Put the finishing touches to the biggest piece of investigative journalism she'd ever done. On the Mafia in France, and in the South. No one had ever dug that deep. Too deep, she realized now. She'd remembered what Bruno had said.

"I'm in trouble. Big trouble."

She'd called him from a phone booth in La Spezia. It was almost one o'clock in the morning. She'd woken him up. He was an early riser, because of the animals. Babette was shaking. Two hours earlier, after driving from Orvieto without stopping, almost like a madwoman, she'd reached Manarola. A town in the Cinque Terre, perched on a rock, where an old friend of Gianni's named Beppe lived. She'd dialed his number, as he'd asked her to. But be careful, he'd said that very morning.

"*Pronto.*"

Babette had hung up. It wasn't Beppe's voice. Then she'd seen the carabinieri arrive in two cars that drew up on the main street. She knew immediately what had happened: the killers had gotten there before her.

She had turned around and gone back the way she had come, along a narrow, twisting mountain road. Hands tight on the wheel, exhausted, but keeping her eyes open for any cars about to overtake her or coming toward her.

"Come," Bruno had said.

She'd found a seedy room in the Hotel Firenze e

Continentale, near the station. She hadn't slept a wink all night. The trains. The presence of death. It all kept coming back to her, down to the smallest detail. A taxi had dropped her on Campo de' Fiori. Gianni had just come back from Palermo. He was waiting for her in his apartment. Ten days is a long time, he'd said on the phone. It had been a long time for her, too. She didn't know if she loved Gianni, but her whole body yearned for him.

"Gianni! Gianni!"

The door was open, but that hadn't worried her.

"Gianni!"

He was there. Tied to a chair. Naked. Dead. She closed her eyes, but too late. She knew she would have to live with that image.

When she'd opened her eyes again, she'd seen the burn marks on his chest, stomach and thighs. No, she didn't want to look. She turned her eyes away from Gianni's mutilated cock. She started screaming. She saw herself screaming, her body frozen rigid, her arms dangling, her mouth wide open. Her screams swelled with the smell of blood, shit and piss that filled the room. When she couldn't breathe anymore, she threw up. At Gianni's feet. Where someone had written in chalk on the wooden floor: *Present for Mademoiselle Bellini. See you later.*

Gianni's older brother Francesco was murdered the morning she left Orvieto. Beppe before she arrived in Manarola.

From now on, she was a hunted woman.

Bruno had been waiting for her at the bus stop in Saint-Jean-du-Gard. This was how she'd gotten there: train from La Spezia to Ventimiglia, rental car through the little border post at Menton, another train to Nîmes, then a bus. Just to be on the safe side. She didn't really think they were following her. They'd be waiting for her in her apartment in Marseilles. That was the logical thing to do. And everything the Mafia did had its own implacable logic. She'd seen plenty of evidence of that over the past two years.

Just before they got to Le Castellas, at a point where the road overhangs the valley, Bruno had stopped his old jeep.

"Come on, let's go for walk."

They'd walked to the cliff edge. You could just about see Le Castellas, about two miles farther up, at the end of a dirt track. It was as far as you could go.

"You're safe here. If anyone comes up, Michel, the park ranger, calls me. And if someone was coming along the ridge, Daniel would tell me. We're still the same, I call four times a day, he calls four times a day. If one of us doesn't call when he's supposed to, it means something's wrong. When Daniel's tractor overturned, that was how I found out."

Babette had looked at him, unable to say a word. Not even thank you.

"And don't feel you're obliged to tell me what kind of trouble you're in."

Bruno had taken her in his arms, and she had started crying.

Babette shivered. The sun had gone down, and the mountains stood out purple against the sky. She carefully stubbed out her cigarette butt with her foot, stood up, and walked down towards Le Castellas. Soothed by the daily miracle of sunset.

In her room, she read over the long letter she'd written to Fabio. In it, she'd told him everything that had happened since she'd arrived in Rome two years earlier. Including how it had ended. How desperate she was. But also how determined. She'd see it through to the end. She'd publish the results of her investigation. In a newspaper, or as a book. *Everything has to come out into the open*, she'd written.

She was still thinking of that beautiful sunset, and wanted

to end the letter with it. She wanted to tell Fabio that, in spite of everything, the sun was more beautiful over the sea, no, not more beautiful but more real, no, that wasn't it either, what she wanted was to be with him in his boat, off Riou, watching the sun melt into the sea.

She tore up the letter. She took a new sheet of paper and wrote *I still love you*. Beneath it, she wrote *Take good care of this for me*, put five computer disks in a padded envelope, sealed it and stood up. It was time for dinner with Bruno and his family.

1.

IN WHICH WHAT PEOPLE HAVE ON THEIR MINDS IS CLEARER THAN WHAT THEY SAY WITH THEIR TONGUES

Life stank of death.

That's what I'd been thinking last night, walking into Hassan's bar, the Maraîchers. It wasn't just one of those vague ideas you get in your head sometimes. No, I really felt death around me. The rotten putrid smell of it. I'd sniffed my arm, and the smell disgusted me. It was the same smell. I also stank of death. "Take it easy, Fabio," I'd told myself. "Go home, take a shower, calm down, take the boat out. A nice cool sea breeze and everything will be fine, you'll see."

The fact is, it was hot. In the upper eighties. The air was a viscous mixture of humidity and pollution. Marseilles was stifling. Easy to work up a thirst. So instead of going straight home through the Vieux-Port and along the Corniche—the most direct route to Les Goudes, where I lived—I'd turned onto the narrow Rue Curiol, at the end of the Canebière. The Bar des Maraîchers was right at the top of the street, near Place Jean Jaurès.

It felt good to be in Hassan's bar. There were no barriers of age, sex, color or class among the regulars there. We were all friends. You could be sure no one who came there for a *pastis* voted for the National Front, or ever had. Not even once, unlike some people I knew. Everyone in this bar knew why they were from Marseilles and not somewhere else, why they lived in Marseilles and not somewhere else. Friendship hung in the air, along with the fumes of anise. We only had to exchange glances to know we were all the children of exiles. There was something reassuring about that. We had nothing to lose, because we'd already lost everything.

When I came in, Léo Ferré was singing:

I sense the arrival
of trains full of Brownings,
Berettas and black flowers
And florists preparing bloodbaths
For the news on color TV . . .

I'd had a *pastis* at the bar, and Hassan had refilled it, as usual. After that, I'd lost count of how many *pastis* I had. At one point, maybe when I was on my fourth, Hassan had leaned towards me.

"Don't you think working class people are a bit clumsy?"

It wasn't a question. It was just an observation. A statement. Hassan wasn't the talkative type. But he liked to come out with little phrases like that to whoever was at the bar. Like a maxim to be pondered.

"What am I supposed to say to that?" I'd replied.

"Nothing. There's nothing to say. We do what we can. That's all. Come on, finish your drink."

The bar had gradually filled up, sending the temperature several degrees higher. Some people went outside to drink, but it wasn't much better there. Night had fallen, but there still wasn't a hint of coolness. The mugginess was overwhelming.

I'd gone out on the sidewalk to talk with Didier Perez. He'd come in to Hassan's and as soon as he saw me had come straight up to me.

"Just the man I wanted to see."

"You're in luck. I was planning to go fishing."

"Shall we go outside?"

It was Hassan who'd introduced me to Perez one night. Perez was a painter. Fascinated by the magic of signs. We were the same age. His parents, originally from Almeria, had emigrated to Algeria after Franco's victory. That's where he was born. When Algeria became independent, none of the family had to think about what their nationality was. They would be Algerians.

Perez had left Algiers in 1993. A teacher at the School of Fine Arts, he was also one of the leaders of the Federation of Algerian Artists, Intellectuals and Scientists. When the death threats became more specific, his friends advised him to go away for a while. He'd been in Marseilles barely a week when he learned that the principal and his son had been murdered inside the school. He decided to stay in Marseilles, with his wife and children.

The thing that had immediately drawn me to him was his passion for the Tuareg. I didn't know the desert, but I knew the sea. To me, they were the same. We'd talked a lot about that. About the earth and the sea, the dust and the stars. One evening, he gave me a delicately moulded ring.

"It's from over there. The combination of points and lines is called the *Khaten*. It tells you what's going to happen to those you love who've gone away, and also what's going to happen to you in the future." Perez had placed the ring in the palm of my hand.

"I think I'd rather not know."

He had laughed. "Don't worry, Fabio. You have to know how to read the signs. The *Khat al R'mel*. Whatever it is, it's not going to happen in a hurry! But if it's written, it's written."

I'd never worn a ring in my life. Not even my father's, after he died. I'd hesitated for a moment, then I'd put the ring on the fourth finger of my left hand. As if to seal my fate once and for all. That night, I'd thought, I was finally old enough.

Out on the sidewalk, with our glasses in our hands, we'd

talked about this and that, then Perez had put his arm around my shoulder. "I need to ask you a favor."

"Go ahead."

"I'm expecting someone from Algeria. Could he stay with you? It'll only be for a week. My place isn't big enough."

He looked straight at me with his dark eyes. My place wasn't all that much bigger. The cottage I'd inherited from my parents had only two rooms. A small bedroom and a big dining room cum kitchen. I'd refurbished the place as best I could. I'd kept things simple, not too much furniture. I felt good there. The terrace looked out onto the sea. At the bottom of a flight of eight steps was the boat, with a pointed stern, that I'd bought from Honorine, my neighbor. Perez knew that. I'd invited him and his wife and friends over for a meal several times.

"I'd feel safe, knowing he was with you," he said.

Now I looked at him. "Of course, Didier. When's he coming?"

"I'm not sure yet. Tomorrow, the day after tomorrow, in a week. I really don't know. It's all a bit complicated. I'll call you."

After he'd left, I'd gone back to my place at the bar and drunk with whoever was around, and with Hassan who was always happy to join in. I listened to the conversations. The music, too. Once the aperitif hour was over, Hassan would abandon Ferré for jazz. He always chose the tracks carefully. As if trying to find a sound to fit the mood of every moment. Death, the smell of it, was receding. No doubt about it, I preferred the smell of anise.

"I prefer the smell of anise," I'd yelled at Hassan.

I was starting to get slightly drunk.

"Sure."

He'd winked at me. He was a real friend. Miles Davis had launched into "Solea." I loved that track. I'd been playing it constantly, at night, ever since Lole had left me.

"The *solea*," she'd explained one evening, "is the back-bone of flamenco singing."

"Why don't you sing? Flamenco, jazz . . ."

I knew she had a great voice. A cousin of hers named Pedro had told me. But Lole had always refused to sing outside family gatherings.

"I haven't yet found what I'm looking for," she'd replied, after a long silence. The same silence you had to find at the most intense moment of the *solea*. "You should have understood that by now, Fabio."

"What should I have understood?"

She'd smiled sadly.

It was in the last few weeks of our life together. One of those nights when we'd tired ourselves out talking until the early hours, chain smoking and drinking Lagavulin.

"Explain it to me, Lole, what should I have understood?"

I'd been aware that she was drifting away from me. A little more with every month that passed. Even her body was less open. The passion had gone from it. Our desires weren't leading anywhere new, just perpetuating an old love affair. Nostalgia for a love that might have been.

"There's nothing to explain, Fabio. That's the tragedy of life. You've been listening to flamenco for years, and you're still asking me what you should have understood."

It was a letter, a letter from Babette, that had set everything in motion. I'd met Babette when I'd been appointed head of the Neighborhood Surveillance Squad in North Marseilles. She was just starting out as a journalist. It just happened to be her that her newspaper, *La Marseillaise*, had asked to interview this rare bird the police were sending to the front line, and we'd become lovers. "Seasonal lovers," she liked to call us. Then one day, we'd become friends. Without ever having said that we loved each other.

Two years ago, she'd met an Italian lawyer named Gianni

Simeone. Love at first sight. She'd followed him to Rome. Knowing her, I was sure love wasn't the only reason. I was right. Simeone's specialty was the Mafia. And for years, ever since she'd gone freelance, Babette's dream had been to write the most in-depth report yet attempted on the influence of the Mafia in the South of France.

Babette had told me all about it—how far she'd gotten with her work, what still remained to be done—when she'd come back to Marseilles to check out a few things in local business and political circles. We'd met three or four times, and talked over a grilled sea bass with fennel, at Paul's on Rue Saint-Saëns. One of the few restaurants in the harbor area, along with L'Oursin, which isn't a tourist trap. What I particularly liked was the way we met as lovers, even though we weren't. But I couldn't have said why. Couldn't have explained it to myself. Much less to Lole.

And when Lole came back from Seville, where she'd been visiting with her mother, I didn't tell her about Babette, or that we'd met a few times. Lole and I had known each other since we were teenagers. She'd loved Ugo. Then Manu. Then me. The last survivor of our dreams. I had no secrets from her. She knew about the women I'd loved and lost. But I'd never talked to her about Babette. Because what there had been between us—what there still was between us—was too complicated.

"Who is this Babette? Why did you tell her you love her?"

She'd opened a letter from Babette. It might have been chance, it might have been jealousy, it doesn't matter. *Why does the word "love" have to be so full of meaning?* Babette had written. *We've both said "I love you."*

"There's 'I love you' and there's 'I love you,'" I'd stammered.

"Say that again."

It was so hard to explain. You could say "I love you" out

of loyalty to a love that never really existed, and you could say "I love you" to express the truth of a relationship built on the thousand joys of everyday life.

I hadn't been frank with her. I'd tried to wriggle out of it, and only ended up digging a deeper hole for myself. And at the end of a beautiful summer night, I'd lost Lole. We were on my terrace, finishing a bottle of white wine from the Cinque Terre. A Vernazza, which some friends of ours had brought back with them.

"You know something?" she'd said. "When you can't live anymore, you have the right to die and make a last spark out of your own death."

Since Lole had left, I'd thought a lot about those words. And I'd been looking desperately for that spark.

"What did you say?" Hassan had asked.

"Did I say something?"

"I thought you did." He'd served another round, then leaned towards me and said, "What people have in their minds is sometimes clearer than what they say with their tongues."

I should have called it a day, finished my drink and gone home. Taken the boat and sailed out to the Riou islands to watch the sun rise. I couldn't stand the thoughts that were going through my head. The smell of death had come back. With my fingertips, I touched the ring Perez had given me. I didn't know if that was a good or a bad omen.

Behind me, a curious conversation had started between a young man and a woman of about forty.

"Shit!" the young man had said, irritably. "You're just like Madame de Merteuil."

"Who's that?"

"A character in a novel. *Les Liaisons dangereuses*."

"Never heard of it. Are you trying to insult me?"

That made me smile, and I asked Hassan to pour me another drink. That was when Sonia came in. Though I didn't know yet that her name was Sonia. She was a woman I'd seen a few times recently. The last time was in June, at a fishermen's festival in L'Estaque. We'd never spoken.

Sonia had made her way through the crowd to the bar and slipped in between another customer and me. Her body up against mine.

"Don't tell me you were looking for me."

"Why?"

"Because someone already said that to me tonight."

Her face lit up in a smile. "I wasn't looking for you. But I'm pleased to see you here."

"So am I! Hassan, give the lady a drink."

"The lady's name is Sonia," he said.

And he poured her a whisky on the rocks. Without asking. As if she were a regular.

"Cheers, Sonia."

We clinked glasses. Sonia's gray-blue eyes met mine. And the night took a different turn. I started getting a hard-on. Such a big one it almost hurt. I'd lost count of how many months it had been, but it was ages since I'd last slept with a woman. I think I'd almost forgotten what it was like to get a hard-on.

Other rounds followed. At the bar, then at a little table that had become free. Sonia's thigh up against mine. Burning me. I remember wondering why things always happen so fast. Falling in love. If only it happened when you were on top form, when you felt ready for the other person. I'd told myself it was impossible to control what happened in your life. I'd told myself a lot of things. But I couldn't remember any of them. Or anything Sonia had told me either.

I couldn't remember anything about the way that night had ended. And the phone was ringing.

*

The phone was ringing, making my temples throb. There was a thunderstorm inside my head. I made a huge effort and opened my eyes. I was lying naked on my bed.

The phone was still ringing. Shit! Why did I always forget to switch on the fucking answering machine?

I rolled over and reached out my arm.

"Yeah?"

"Montale." A loathsome voice.

"You've got the wrong number," I said, and hung up.

Less than a minute later, the phone rang again. The same loathsome voice. With a hint of an Italian accent.

"You see, it's the right number. Or would you rather we paid you a visit?"

This wasn't the kind of awakening I'd been dreaming of. But the guy's voice hit my body like an ice-cold shower. It sent a chill through me. I knew voices like that, I knew the kind of face that went with them, the kind of body, I even knew where they kept their guns.

I ordered the noise inside my head to stop. "I'm listening."

"I have one question for you. Do you know the whereabouts of Babette Bellini?"

I wasn't in an ice-cold shower anymore. I was at the North Pole. I started shivering. I pulled up the sheet and wrapped it around me.

"Who is this?"

"Don't fuck around, Montale. Your girlfriend, the shit-stirrer, Babette. Do you know where she is?"

"She was in Rome," I said, telling myself that if they were looking for her here it must mean she wasn't down there any more.

"She's not there anymore."

"She must have forgotten to tell me."

"Interesting," the guy sneered.

There was silence. A silence so heavy, my ears started buzzing.

"Is that all?"

"Here's the deal, Montale. You do whatever you have to do, but you find your girlfriend for us. She has some things that belong to us and we'd like them back. Since you don't have anything to do all fucking day, it shouldn't take long, should it?"

"Go fuck yourself!"

"By the time I call you again, you won't be so high and mighty, Montale." He hung up.

I'd been right. Life did stink of death.

2.

IN WHICH JUST BECAUSE YOU'RE USED TO LIFE DOESN'T MEAN YOU HAVE TO CARRY ON LIVING

On the table, next to my car keys, Sonia had left a note. *You were too plastered. A pity. Call me tonight. Bye.* Then her telephone number. Ten winning numbers. An invitation to happiness.

Sonia. I smiled, remembering her gray-blue eyes, her burning hot thigh against mine. And the way her face lit up when she smiled. They were my only memories of her, but they were good ones. I couldn't wait until tonight. Neither could my cock, straining inside my underwear just to think about it.

My head felt as heavy as a mountain. I hesitated between taking a shower and making coffee. It had to be coffee. And a cigarette. The first drag tore my insides out. I thought they were going to come out through my mouth. "Shit!" I said, and took another drag, for the sake of it. I heaved again, more violently than the first time, and the throbbing in my head started up again, louder than ever.

I stood bent double over the kitchen sink, but there was nothing to throw up. Not even my lungs. Not yet! In the old days, I used to inhale an appetite for life with the first drag of the first cigarette. Those days were long gone. The demons inside my chest didn't have much to feed on anymore. Just because you're used to life doesn't mean you have to carry on living. I was reminded of that every morning when I felt like throwing up.

I put my head under the cold water faucet, screamed a bit, then stretched and got my breath back. I hadn't let go of the cigarette, and it was burning my fingers. I hadn't been doing enough sports lately. Hadn't gone walking in the *calanques*.

Hadn't done any training at Mavros's gym. Good food, alcohol, cigarettes. "In ten years, Montale, you'll be dead," I told myself. "Do something, for fuck's sake!" I thought again about Sonia. It felt really good to think about her. Then her image was replaced by Babette's.

Where was Babette? What the hell kind of trouble was she in? The guy on the phone hadn't just been trying to scare me. There'd been a real threat in every word. The cold way he'd uttered them. I stubbed out the cigarette and lit another as I poured out the coffee. I gulped down some of it, took a long drag on the cigarette, and went out on the terrace.

The burning sun beat down on me, blinding me. My whole body broke out in a sweat. I felt dizzy. I thought for a moment I was going to pass out. But I didn't. The floor of the terrace steadied itself. I opened my eyes. The one real gift that life gave me every day was right there in front of me. The sea and the sky. As far as the eye could see. And that light that was like no other, that passed from one to the other. I'd often thought that holding a woman's body was a way of holding on to that same ineffable joy that came down from the sky to the sea.

Had I held Sonia's body against me last night? Sonia had come back with me, but how had she left? Was she the one who'd undressed me? Had she slept here? With me? Had we made love? No. No, you were too plastered. She told you that in her note.

Honorine's voice interrupted my thoughts. "Hey, don't you know what time it is?"

I turned to face her. Honorine. My old Honorine. She was the only thing left of my burned-out world. Loyal to the end. She was almost at the age when you didn't get any older. She shrank a little more every year, but her face was only slightly wrinkled, as if the blows she'd taken in her life had slid off her without really touching her, without shaking the joy she felt at living in this world. "It's good to be alive, just to have seen these things," she often said, pointing to the sky and the sea in front of us, with the islands in the background. "Just for that, I don't regret being born. In spite of all the things that have happened to me . . ." She always broke off there. As if she didn't want to allow a tinge of sadness to spoil her simple joy in living. Honorine had only happy memories now. I loved her. She was the greatest of all mothers. And she was all mine.

She opened the little gate separating her terrace from mine, and walked toward me with her shopping bag in her hand, shuffling a little but still stepping confidently. "It's almost noon, you know!"

I made a sweeping gesture, taking in the sea and the sky. "I'm on vacation."

"Only people who work take vacations."

That had been Honorine's obsession for the past few months. To find me work. To get me to look for work. She couldn't stand the idea of a man "who's still young, like you" doing nothing all day.

It fact, that wasn't entirely true. Every afternoon, from two to seven, I took Fonfon's place in his bar. I'd been doing it for more than a year now. Fonfon had planned to close his bar. To sell it. But when it came to it, he couldn't do it. He'd spent too many years serving his customers, talking to them, arguing with them. Closing down would have been like dying. One morning, he'd offered to sell me his bar. For the symbolic sum of one franc.

"That way," he'd said, "I'll be able to come in from time to time and lend you a hand. At aperitif time, for instance. You know, just to have something to do."

I'd refused. He could keep his bar, and I'd be the one to come in and give him a hand.

"All right, then, in the afternoons."

We'd agreed on that. It gave me a little extra money to pay for gas, smokes, and occasional nights on the town. I still had about a hundred thousand francs stashed away. It wasn't much, and the money didn't last long, but at least I could plan ahead. Quite a long way ahead, in fact. My needs were few, and getting fewer. The worst thing that could happen to me was that my old Renault 5 would break down, and I'd be forced to buy another car.

"Honorine, don't start on that again."

She frowned at me and pursed her lips. She was trying to look severe, but her eyes gave her away. They were full of love. She only shouted at me because she loved me and was afraid something bad would happen to me if I just stayed here, doing nothing. The devil makes work for idle hands, everyone knows that. She'd drummed that into us often enough, in the days when Ugo, Manu and I used to hang out here. We'd reply by quoting Baudelaire's *Les Fleurs du Mal* at her. Happiness, luxury, calm and sensuality. That was when she'd shout at us. I had only to look at her eyes to know if she was angry or not.

Maybe she should really have shouted at us. But Honorine wasn't our mother. How could she have guessed that after all our fooling around, we'd end up doing something really foolish? To her, we were just kids, no better and no worse than any others. And we always had lots of books with us. From her terrace, she could hear us reading aloud, facing the sea as the sun went down. Honorine had always believed that books made you wise, intelligent, serious. Not that it could lead to holding up drugstores and gas stations. And shooting people.

There'd been real anger in her eyes the day, thirty years ago, when I'd come to say goodbye to her. She was so angry, it left her speechless. I'd just signed on for five years in the Colonial Army and was on my way to Djibouti. To get away from Marseilles. And my life. Because Ugo and Manu had crossed the line. Manu had gone crazy and shot a druggist on Rue des Trois-Mages during a hold-up. The next day, I'd read in the newspaper that the man, who had a wife and children, would be paralyzed for life. I was horrified by what we'd done.

Ever since that night, I'd hated guns. Becoming a policeman had made no difference. I'd never gotten used to carrying a weapon. I'd often talked to my colleagues about it. I knew, of course, you could always come up against a rapist, a maniac, a gangster. There were plenty of people out there—violent, crazy or just desperate—who might cross our path one day. That was something that had happened to me a few times. But at the end of that path, I always saw Manu, with his gun in his hand. And Ugo behind him. And myself, somewhere in the vicinity.

Manu had been killed by mobsters. Ugo by cops. I was still alive. That meant I'd been lucky. Lucky to have seen in the looks some adults gave me that we were men. Human beings. And that it wasn't up to us to take life.

Honorine picked up her shopping bag. "You know, talking to you is like talking to a deaf man."

She started walking back to her terrace. When she reached the gate, she turned to look at me. "Hey, how about I open a jar of sweet peppers for lunch? With a few anchovies. I'll make a big salad. In this heat . . ."

I smiled. "I'd be fine with a tomato omelette."

"What's the matter with you men today? That's all Fonfon wanted as well."

"We got together on the phone."

"Go on, make fun of me!"

For several months, Honorine had been cooking for Fonfon, too. The three of us often ate together on my terrace in the evenings. In fact, Fonfon and Honorine were spending more and more time together. A few days before, Fonfon had even come over to her place for an afternoon nap. When he got back to the bar, around five o'clock, he'd looked as embarrassed as a kid who's just kissed a girl for the first time.

I was the one who'd helped Fonfon and Honorine to get together. I didn't think it was right they should both be alone. They'd stayed faithful to their dear departed for nearly fifteen years. Quite long enough, in my opinion. There was no shame in not wanting to end your days alone.

One Sunday morning, I'd suggested the three of us go to the Frioul islands for a picnic. Honorine had taken a lot of persuading. She hadn't even been on the boat since her husband, Toinou, had died.

"Dammit, Honorine!" I'd said, getting a little irritated. "Since I've had this boat, I've only ever taken Lole out. I'm taking both of you now, because I love you. Both of you, can't you get that into your head?"

Her eyes had misted over, then she'd smiled. That was when I knew that, without in any way repudiating her life with Toinou, she was finally turning the page. On the way back from the picnic, she'd held Fonfon's hand, and I'd heard her say to him in a low voice, "We can die happy now, can't we?"

"Oh, I think we still have a little time left, don't you?" he'd replied.

I'd turned away and looked out to the horizon. To where the sea was darker and thicker. I'd told myself that the solution to all the contradictions of life was there, in that sea. My Mediterranean. And I'd seen myself melting into it, at last resolving all the things I'd never managed to resolve in my life, and never would.

The love those two old people felt for each other had made me cry.

At the end of the meal, Honorine, who'd been strangely quiet throughout, said, "Tell me, that brunette who brought you home last night, is she coming back? Sonia, wasn't it?"

I was surprised. "I don't know," I stammered, almost nervously. "Why?"

"Because she seems really nice. I thought . . ."

That was another of Honorine's obsessions. She wanted me to find myself a woman. A nice woman, who'd take care of me, even though the thought of another woman cooking for me instead of her turned her stomach.

I don't know how many times I'd explained to her that the only woman in my life was Lole. Lole had left because I couldn't be the man she'd expected me to be. There was no doubt about it anymore. And the way I'd hurt her the most was in forcing her to go. Forcing her to leave me. It often woke me up at night. The way I'd hurt her. The way I'd hurt us.

But I'd been waiting for Lole my whole life, and I wasn't going to give her up that easily. I needed to believe she'd come back. That we'd start all over again. That our dreams, our old dreams, which had brought us together again and given us so much joy already, could at last be fulfilled. Simply and freely. With no more fears or doubts. A relationship based on trust.

Whenever I said that, Honorine would look at me sadly. She knew that Lole had a new life now, in Seville. With a guitarist, who'd crossed over from flamenco to jazz. In the great tradition of Django Reinhardt. Something like Bireli Lagrene. She'd finally agreed to sing for the *gajos*. She'd joined her friend's band about a year ago, done gigs with them. They'd recorded an album together. An album of jazz standards. She'd sent it to me, with a note saying only, *How are you?*

I can't give you anything but love, baby . . . I hadn't gotten any farther than that first track. Not that it wasn't good. On the contrary. Her voice was soft and husky. I recognized the way it had sounded sometimes when we made love. But it wasn't Lole's voice I heard, only the guitar supporting it. Making it seem even richer. I couldn't bear it. I'd put away the album, but I couldn't put away my stupid illusions so easily.

"Did you talk?" I asked Honorine.

"Sure we did. We had coffee together." She gave me a big smile. "The poor girl wasn't in a very fit state to go to work."

I didn't know what to say. I had no image of Sonia's body. Her naked body. I only knew that the thin dress she'd been wearing last night promised all kinds of happiness to a decent man. But maybe I wasn't such a decent man after all.

"Fonfon called Alex. You know, the cab driver who sometimes plays cards with the two of you. To drive her back. I think she was a little late."

Life went on. It always did.

"And what did you and Sonia talk about?"

"A bit about her. Quite a lot about you. We weren't dishing the dirt, or anything. We just talked."

She folded her napkin and looked me in the eyes. As she had done earlier on the terrace. But without the wicked gleam. "She told me you were unhappy."

"Unhappy!" I forced myself to laugh, and lit a cigarette, trying to look composed. What the hell could I have told Sonia? I felt like a little kid caught doing something wrong.

"She hardly knows me."

"That's why I said she's nice. Realizing that about you in such a short time together. It was a short time, wasn't it?"

"Yes, it was a short time." I stood up. "I'm going to Fonfon's to have a coffee."

"What is this, we can't talk anymore?" She was angry.

"I'm sorry, Honorine. I didn't get much sleep."

"It's all right. All I said was, I'd like to see her again." The wicked gleam was back in her eyes.

"So would I, Honorine. I'd like to see her again too."

3.

IN WHICH IT ISN'T POINTLESS TO HAVE A FEW ILLUSIONS ABOUT LIFE

Fonfon had shrugged when I told him, as I drank my coffee, that I couldn't look after the bar that afternoon. I kept thinking about the mess Babette seemed to have gotten herself in. I had to find out where she was. In her case, that wasn't so easy. For all I knew, she might be cruising on an Arab emir's yacht. Pure speculation, of course. Best case scenario. In fact, the more I thought about it, the more convinced I was that she was on the run. Or in hiding somewhere.

I'd decided to check out the apartment she'd kept at the top of Cours Julien. She'd bought it for next to nothing in the seventies and now she was worth a fortune. Cours Julien was the hottest neighborhood in Marseilles. Nothing but restaurants, bars, cafés with live music, antique shops and fashion stores on both sides of the street, all the way up to the Notre Dame du Mont subway station. From seven onwards, it was the center of Marseilles nightlife.

"I knew it wouldn't last," Fonfon had grunted.

"Fonfon, it's just this once."

"O.K. . . . Anyway, there won't be many customers. They'll all have their asses in the water. Another coffee?"

"If it's not too much trouble."

"Don't make that face! I'm only teasing. I don't know what the girls are doing to you these days, but when you get out of bed in the morning, you look like you've been run over by a steamroller."

"It's not the girls, it's the *pastis*. I lost count last night."

"When I said the girls, I meant the one I put in a taxi this morning."

"Sonia."

"Sonia, that's it. She seems nice."

"Hold on, Fonfon! Don't you start now. Honorine already said that, no need to exaggerate."

"I'm not exaggerating. I'm just telling you the way I see it. And instead of gallivanting off God knows where in this heat, you should do what I'm doing and take a nap. That way, tonight . . ."

"You're shutting the bar?"

"Can you see me waiting all damned afternoon for someone to come in and order a peppermint cordial? Why should I bother? Same tomorrow. And the day after. While this heat lasts, there's no point in making your life a misery. So take some time off, my friend. Go on, go to bed."

I hadn't listened to Fonfon. I should have. I was exhausted. I pulled out a cassette by Mongo Santamaria and put it in the deck. *Mambo Terrifico*. At full volume. And I stepped on the accelerator, just to let a little fresh air into the car. But even with all the windows open, I was streaming with sweat. The beaches, from the Pointe-Rouge to the Rond-Point de David, were packed. Everyone in Marseilles was there, with their asses in the water, like Fonfon had said. He was right to close the bar. Even the movie theatres, which were air conditioned, weren't opening until five.

Less than half an hour later, I parked outside Babette's building. Summer in Marseilles is great. No traffic in town, no parking problems. I rang Madame Orsini's bell. She cleaned Babette's apartment when she was away, made sure everything was all right, and forwarded her mail. I'd phoned to make sure she was in.

"I'm not going anywhere, in this heat. Come any time you like."

She opened the door. You couldn't be sure of Madame

Orsini's age. It could have been anywhere between fifty and sixty. Depending on the hour of the day. Bleached blonde hair, not very tall, a little on the plump side. She was wearing a thin, loose-fitting dress, and when she stood against the light you could see the outline of her body. Judging by the look she gave me, I didn't think she'd have minded taking a little nap with me. I knew why Babette liked her. She was a maneater, too.

"Would you like something to drink?"

"No, thanks. Just the keys to the apartment."

"That's a pity." She smiled, and I smiled back. She handed me the keys. "I haven't heard from Babette in a while."

"She's fine," I lied. "Working hard."

"Is she still in Rome?"

"Yes, with her lawyer."

Madame Orsini looked at me in a curious way. "Oh . . . Oh, yes."

I climbed six floors, and stopped outside Babette's door to catch my breath. The apartment was just as I remembered it. Magnificent. A huge picture window looking out over the Vieux-Port. With the islands of the Frioul in the distance. It was the first thing you saw when you came in, and it was so beautiful it took your breath away. I drank my fill. Because the rest of the place wasn't a pleasant sight. The apartment had been turned upside down. Someone had gotten there before me.

I broke out in a sweat. It was the heat, and the sudden presence of evil. The air became unbreathable. I went to the faucet in the kitchen, let the water run, and drank a big gulp of it.

I walked through the rooms. They had all been searched—thoroughly, it seemed to me, but not carefully. In the bedroom, I sat down on Babette's bed and lit a cigarette. I needed to think.

What I was looking for didn't exist. Babette was so unpredictable that even if she'd left an address book, I would simply have gotten lost in a maze of names, streets, towns and countries. The guy on the phone had come here first, before calling me. I was sure it was him. Them. The Mafia. The killers. They were looking for her and, like me, they'd started at the beginning. With where she lived. They must have found something that had pointed them in my direction. Then I remembered Madame Orsini's questions about Babette. And the way she'd looked at me. They'd been to see her, I was sure of that, too.

I stubbed out my cigarette in a hideous ashtray that said *Ricordo di Roma*. Madame Orsini owed me an explanation. I walked through the apartment again, as if hoping for a bright idea.

In the room Babette used as an office, I noticed two thick ring binders on the floor. I opened the first one. All the stories Babette had covered. Arranged by year. That was just like her. The sense that she was creating something durable. Her life's work. I smiled. And found myself skimming through the pages, going back through the years. Back to the day in March 1988 when she had come to interview me.

Her article was there. Half a page, with my photo in the middle, spread over two columns.

"Stop and search operations are commonplace," I'd said in answer to her first question. *"They're one of the things that foster feelings of rebelliousness in some young people, especially those young people who are experiencing the worst social deprivation. Police harassment legitimizes or reinforces a tendency toward delinquency, contributing to a situation in which young people are without guidelines and become chronically rebellious.*

"Some young people start to feel they are all-powerful, which leads them to reject all authority and attempt to lay down the

law in their projects. To them, the police are a symbol of this authority. But, in order to combat delinquency effectively, police conduct must be above reproach. Rap has become a means of expression for young people in the projects, for the very reason that it often attacks police harassment. In doing so, it shows that we still have a long way to go."

My chiefs hadn't exactly appreciated my tirade. But they hadn't batted an eyelid. They knew my views. That was why they'd put me in charge of the Neighborhood Surveillance Squad in North Marseilles. There had been two major police blunders in quick succession. Lahaouri Ben Mohammed, a seventeen-year-old, had been killed during a routine identity check. There'd been trouble in the projects following that. Then, a few months later, the same thing had happened to another young man, Christian Dovero, the son of a taxi driver. This time the whole city was up in arms. "A Frenchman, dammit!" my superior had screamed. Calm had to be restored urgently. Even before Internal Affairs was called in. The prefecture had decided we needed to act differently, and talk differently. That was when they pulled me out of the hat. The miracle man.

It took me a while to realize that I was merely a puppet being manipulated. They were just waiting to get back to the tried and tested methods. The harassment, the beatings. To please those who clamored for greater security.

Now they'd gone back to those tried and tested methods. And twenty percent of the workforce voted for the National Front. The situation in North Marseilles had turned tense again. And was getting tenser every day. You just had to open the morning paper. Schools ransacked in Saint-André, attacks on night doctors in La Savine, or on municipal employees in La Castellane, night bus drivers threatened. And all the while, heroin, crack, and all that kind of crap were proliferating in the projects, making the kids feel they could do anything.

And driving them crazy. "The two scourges of Marseilles," the rappers of the band IAM kept crying, "are heroin and the National Front." Anyone who'd spent any time among the young knew the explosion was coming.

I'd quit. I knew it was no solution. But you couldn't change the police overnight, in Marseilles or anywhere else. Whether you liked it or not, being a cop meant you had a history behind you. The roundup of Jews in the Vel' d'Hiv. The Algerians thrown in the Seine in October '61. A whole lot of things that had belatedly been admitted—though not yet officially. A whole lot of things that affected the way many cops dealt with the children of immigrants on a daily basis.

I'd long thought the same thing. And I'd started down what my colleagues called the slippery slope. Trying too hard to understand. To explain. To convince. "The youth counselor," they nicknamed me at the neighborhood station house. When I was stripped of my functions, I told my chief that playing on people's subjective feelings of insecurity, instead of pursuing the objective goal of arresting the guilty, was a dangerous path to go down. He barely smiled. He didn't want to have anything more to do with me.

These days, admittedly, the government was singing a different tune. They'd recognized that security wasn't just a question of manpower and resources, but a question of methods. I was somewhat reassured to hear it said, finally, that security wasn't an ideology, and that social reality had to be taken into account. But it was too late for me. I'd left the force and I'd never go back, even though I didn't know how to do anything else.

I wanted to look through the article properly. As I took it out of its sleeve and unfolded it, a small sheet of yellowing paper fell out. On it, Babette had written: *Montale. Lots of charm, intelligent too.* I smiled. Good old Babette! I'd called her after the interview appeared. To thank her for quoting me accurately. She'd invited me to dinner. I guess she already had an ulterior motive. Why deny it? I was only too happy to accept—she was a real looker. But I never imagined that a young journalist would have any interest in seducing a cop who wasn't so young anymore.

Yes, I had to admit as I looked at my photo again, that Montale had lots of charm. I pulled a long face. That was a long time ago. Nearly ten years. My features were thicker and heavier now, and there were lines at the corners of my eyes and down my cheeks. The more time passed, the more worried I was by what I saw in the mirror every morning. Not only was I aging—which was only normal—it seemed to me I was aging badly. I'd talked about it to Lole one night.

"What on earth are you dreaming up now?" she'd retorted.

I wasn't dreaming anything up.

"Do you think I'm good-looking?"

I couldn't remember what she'd replied. In her head, she'd already left. For another life. Another man, in another place. A life that would be beautiful. A man who'd be good-looking.

Later, I'd seen a photo of her friend in a magazine—even in my head, I didn't dare speak the guy's name—and yes, he was good-looking. Thin, with a gaunt face, bushy hair, sparkling eyes, and a nice mouth, rather pursed to my taste, but nice all the same. The opposite of me. I'd hated that photo, especially when I thought of Lole putting it in her billfold instead of mine. That had really hurt. You're jealous, I'd told myself. It was a feeling I hated. But yes, I was jealous. And I felt sick at heart just thinking of Lole taking that photo, or another one, out of her billfold and looking at it, whenever he was away from her for a few days, or even just for a few hours.

It was one of those damned nights when you lie awake in bed and everything is magnified out of all proportion and you can't think properly, can't see straight. It had happened several times before, with other women. But never so painfully, so intensely. Lole was leaving, and my life would lose all meaning. Had already lost all meaning

My photo was looking back at me. I needed a beer. We're only good looking in other people's eyes. In the eyes of the person who loves us. One day, you can't tell the other person he or she is good-looking anymore, because love has gone and you're not desirable yourself. Then you can put on your nicest shirt, cut your hair, grow your moustache, it won't make any difference. All you'll get is "Oh, it suits you" instead of what you're really hoping for, which is "You look so handsome"— words that promise pleasure and rumpled sheets.

I put the article back in its sleeve and closed the binder. I felt suffocated. I lingered for a moment in front of the mirror at the entrance. I seemed to hear Sonia's laughter. Did I still have any of my charm left? Did I still have a future as a lover? I pulled a long face, the way only I knew how. Then I turned and picked up Babette's binders. Reading her articles, I told myself, would take my mind off things.

"I decided I'd like a beer after all," I said as soon as Madame Orsini opened the door.

"Oh. O.K."

This time there was no innuendo in her voice, and she was avoiding my eyes.

"I don't know if it's cold."

"It doesn't matter."

We were face to face. I was holding the keys to Babette's apartment in my hand.

"Did you find what you were looking for?" she asked, jutting her chin at the two binders.

"Maybe."

"Oh."

The silence that followed was heavy and damp.

"Is she in any trouble?" Madame Orsini asked at last.

"What makes you think that?"

"The police came. I don't like that."

"The police?"

Another silence, as stifling as before. I had the taste of the first mouthful of beer in my mouth. She was avoiding my eyes again. There was a hint of fear deep in hers.

"Yes, they showed me their badges."

She was lying.

"And they asked you questions. Where's Babette? Have you seen her lately? Do you know if she has any friends in Marseilles? That kind of thing."

"That kind of thing, yes."

"And you gave them my name and phone number."

"You know how it is with the police."

Now she really wanted me to go. To close the door and leave her alone. There was sweat on her forehead. Cold sweat.

"The police, huh?"

"I don't like to get involved with that kind of thing, you know. I'm not the concierge. I only do it to help Babette out. It's not as if she pays me a lot."

"Did they threaten you?"

This time she looked at me. Startled by my question, and scared by its implications. They had threatened her.

"Yes."

"Did they ask you for my name?"

"They want me to keep an eye on the apartment . . . Let them know if anyone comes, and who. And they told me not to forward the mail. They're going to call me every day, they said. And I'd be well advised to answer."

The phone rang. It was right next to us, on a small table, with a little lace doily under it. Madame Orsini lifted the receiver. I saw her face turn white. She looked at me in panic.

"Yes. Yes, of course."

She placed her trembling hand over the receiver. "It's them. It's . . . it's for you."

She handed me the phone.

"Yes?"

"So you got straight down to work, Montale. That's good. But you're wasting your time there. We're in a hurry, you see?"

"Fuck you."

"No, it's you who's going to get fucked. And soon, asshole!"

He hung up.

Madame Orsini was looking at me. She was terrified now.

"Do what they asked you," I said.

I wanted Sonia. Sonia's smile. Her eyes. Her body, which I still didn't know. I was desperate for her. I wanted to lose myself in her. To forget all the corruption that was blighting our lives.

I still had a few illusions left.

4.

IN WHICH TEARS ARE THE ONLY CURE FOR HATE

I had a beer, then another, and another. I was sitting in the shade on the terrace of La Samaritaine, down by the harbor. At least here there was a little breeze from the sea. It wasn't exactly cool, but it kept me from dripping with sweat every time I took a swig of beer. It felt good to be here. On the finest terrace in the Vieux-Port. The only one that lets you enjoy the light of the city all day long. Nobody who's indifferent to its light will ever understand Marseilles. Down here, you can almost touch it. Even at the hottest times. Even when it forces you to keep your eyes down. Like today.

I ordered another beer, then went off to phone Sonia again. It was nearly eight o'clock, and I'd been calling her every half hour without getting any answer.

The more time passed, the more I wanted to see her. I didn't even know her, but I already missed her. What could she have told Honorine and Fonfon to win them over the way she had? What could she have told me to get me in such a state? How could a woman get inside a man's heart so easily, just with looks and smiles? Was it possible to touch the heart without even touching the skin? That must have been what seduction meant. To affect another person's heart, make it quiver, become attached to it. Sonia.

Her phone was ringing, and still nobody was answering. I was getting desperate. I felt like a teenager in love, who can't wait to hear his girlfriend's voice. I supposed that was one of the reasons cell phones were so popular. Being connected to the person you love, anywhere, at any time. Being able to say to her, yes, I love you, yes, I miss you, yes, see you tonight. But

I couldn't see myself getting a cell phone, and I couldn't understand the way I was feeling about Sonia. The truth was, I couldn't even remember the sound of her voice.

I walked back to my table, and started in on Babette's articles again. I'd already read six of them. They were all about law and order, the projects, the police. And the Mafia. Especially the most recent ones. For the newspaper *Aujourd'hui*, Babette had written an account of the press conference given in Geneva by seven European judges: Renaud Van Ruymbecke from France, Bernard Bertossa from Switzerland, Gherardo Colombo and Edmondo Bruti Liberati from Italy, Baltazar Garzon Real and Carlos Jimenez Villarejo from Spain and Benoît Dejemeppe from Belgium. The title of the article, which had appeared in October 1996, was "Seven Judges Speak Out Against Corruption."

The judges, Babette wrote, expressed their anger at the fact that legal cooperation is either non-existent or is hampered by politicians, that it costs a criminal organization only 200,000 dollars to launder 20 million, and that drug money (1,500 billion francs every year) circulates freely around the world, with 90% of it being reinvested in the Western economies.

Babette reported Bernard Bertossa, public prosecutor of Geneva, as saying, *"It is time to create a Europe governed by the rule of law, in which we have not only the free circulation of criminals and their funds but also the free circulation of evidence."*

But the judges know that, however much they raise the alarm, their efforts are stymied by the schizophrenic attitudes of European governments. "We have to do away with tax havens, which only exist to launder dirty money! We cannot make rules and at the same time provide the means for criminals to get around them!" That is the opinion of Judge Baltazar Garzon Real, who knows that every time a trail leads him to Gibraltar, Andorra, or Monaco, it hits a dead end. "All they have to do these days is set up fake Panamanian companies," says Renaud van Ruymbecke. "The more of these buffer companies there are, the less we can do, even though we know full well that drug money is involved."

Night was falling, but it wasn't getting any cooler. I was sick to the teeth of reading and waiting. At this rate, I'd be plastered again by the time I saw Sonia. If she finally deigned to answer.

Fifteen minutes later, I tried again. Still nothing.

I called Hassan.

"How are you feeling?" he asked.

In the background, Léo Ferré was singing:

> *When the machine has started to hum*
> *When you don't really know where you are*
> *And you wait for whatever will come . . .*

"Feeling fine. Why shouldn't I be?"

"Seeing the state you were in last night."

"Did I make a fool of myself?"

"Never seen anyone who could knock them back and stay calm the way you can."

"You're a good man, Hassan!"

> *And you wait for whatever will come . . .*

"Nice girl, that Sonia."

Even Hassan was getting in on the act.

"Right," I said. "Talking of Sonia, any idea where she lives?"

"Let me see . . ." he said, taking a swig of something. "Rue Consolat. 24 or 26, I'm not sure. But it's an even number, that I can tell you. I can never remember odd numbers." He laughed, and took another swig.

"What are you on right now?" I asked, out of curiosity.

"Beer."

"Me, too. What's her surname?"

"De Luca."

An Italian. Shit. It had been ages. Since Babette, I'd avoided Italian women.

"You met her father here a couple of times. Used to be a longshoreman. Attilio. Know the one I mean? Not very tall. Bald."

"Yes, of course. He's her father?"

"Yup." Another swig. "So if I see this Sonia, I'll tell her you're making inquiries about her, shall I?"

He laughed again. I didn't know what time he'd started, but he was on good form.

"Sure. See you one of these nights. Ciao."

Sonia lived at No. 28.

I rang the bell at the entrance. The door opened. My heart started pounding. On the letter box, it said *1st floor*. I climbed the stairs, four steps at a time. I knocked a couple of times. The door opened. And closed behind me.

Two men stood there looking at me. One of them showed me his badge.

"Police. Who are you?"

"What are you doing here?"

My heart was pounding again. For a different reason this time. I imagined the worst. Of course, I thought, as soon as you turn your head away, even if it's only for a moment, life gets ready to play its dirty tricks on you. Layer upon layer. Like a napoleon. A layer of cream, a layer of broken pastry. Broken life. Fuck. No, I couldn't imagine the worst. But I could guess what it was. My heart stopped beating. The smell of death had come back. Not the one that had been floating around in my head, that I'd thought I could feel on me. No, the real smell of death. The smell of blood, too. They often go together.

"I asked you a question."

"Montale. Fabio Montale. I was supposed to meeting Sonia." It was only half a lie.

"I'm going downstairs, Alain," the other cop said. He looked white.

"O.K., Bernard. They'll be here soon."

"What's going on?" I said, to put my mind at rest.

"You're her . . ." He looked me up and down. Trying to guess my age, and Sonia's. A good twenty years' difference, he must have concluded. "Her friend?"

"Yes. A friend."

"Montale, you said?" He seemed to be thinking about something. Then he looked at me again.

"Yes. Fabio Montale."

"She's dead. Murdered."

I felt a knot in my stomach, a hard, heavy lump forming in the pit of my stomach and starting to move up and down my body. Moving all the way up to my throat. Choking me. Leaving me speechless. Without anything to say. As if all words had gone back to prehistory. Back to the caves, from which mankind should never have emerged. In the beginning was the worst. The primal scream of the first man. A scream of despair, beneath the starry vault. Despair at realizing that one day, in spite of all that beauty, one day, he would kill his brother. In the beginning were all the reasons to kill. Even before there were names for them. Envy, jealousy. Desire, fear. Money. Power. Hate. Hate toward others. Hate toward the world.

Hate.

I wanted to cry out. To scream.

Sonia.

Hate. The lump stopped rising and falling. The blood drained from my veins and gathered in that lump, heavy now in my stomach. An icy cold overcame me. Hate. I'd have to live with the cold, and the hate. Sonia.

"Sonia," I murmured.

"Are you all right?" the cop asked.

"No."

"Sit down."

I sat down. In an armchair I didn't know. In an apartment I didn't know. The apartment of a woman I didn't know. A woman who was dead. Murdered. Sonia.

"How?" I asked.

The cop offered me a cigarette.

"Thanks," I said, and lit it.

"Her throat was cut. In the shower."

"A sex maniac?"

He shrugged. That meant no. Or at least maybe not. If she'd been raped, he'd have said raped and murdered. He'd only said murdered.

"I used to be a cop, too. A long time ago."

"Montale . . . I thought so . . . North Marseilles, right?" He held out his hand. "I'm Béraud. Alain Béraud. You didn't have many friends . . ."

"I know. Only one. Loubet."

"Loubet. Yeah . . . He was transferred. Six months ago."

"Uh-huh."

"Saint-Brieuc, in Brittany. Not exactly a promotion."

"I can imagine."

"He didn't have many friends, either."

We heard a police siren. The team was arriving. They'd be searching for fingerprints. Photographing the crime scene. The body. Analyzing. Questioning. Taking statements. All routine. Just one more crime.

"How about you?"

"I worked for him. For six months. It was O.K. He was a straight guy."

Outside, the siren was still screaming. The police van probably couldn't find a parking space. Rue Consolat was a narrow street, and everyone parked wherever they liked, however they liked.

It was doing me good to talk. It was a way of keeping at bay the images of Sonia with her throat cut that were starting to flood into my head. A flood I couldn't control. Like those sleepless nights, when you keep playing over and over, like a movie in your head, images of the woman you love in another man's arms, kissing him, smiling at him, reaching orgasm, whispering, it's good, yes, it's so good. It's the same face. The same spasms of pleasure. The same sighs. The same words. Only another man's lips. Another man's hands. Another man's cock.

Lola was gone.

And Sonia was dead. Murdered.

The gaping wound, with thick, clotted blood oozing out over her breast, her stomach, forming a little pool in her navel, then oozing down between her thighs and over her cunt. The images were there, as horrible as they always were. And the water from the shower washing the blood into the city's sewers . . .

Sonia. Why?

Why was I always on the side of life where everything was cold and tragic? Was there a reason for it? Or was it just chance? Was it because I didn't love life enough?

"Montale?"

The questions were mounting up. And with them, all the images of corpses I'd stored in my head since the days when I was a cop. Hundreds of corpses of strangers. And the others. The people I loved. Manu, Ugo. Guitou, so young. And Leila. Leila, so wonderfully beautiful. I'd never been there to prevent their deaths.

Always too late, Montale. Late for death. Late for life, too. For friendship. For love.

Out of sync, lost. Always.

And now Sonia.

"Montale?"

And hate.

"Yes," I said.

I'd take the boat out. I'd head for the open sea. In the darkness. To ask questions of the silence. And spit at the stars, as the first man must have done, coming home one night after a day's hunting to find his wife with her throat cut.

"We have to take your statement."

"Yes," I said. "How . . . How did you find out?"

"The daycare center."

"What daycare center?"

I took out my cigarettes and offered one to Béraud. He refused. He pulled a chair over and sat down facing me. His tone was less friendly now.

"She has a son. Enzo. He's eight years old. Didn't you know?"

"I only met her last night."

"Where?"

"In a bar. Les Maraîchers. I'm a regular there. So was she, apparently. But we never met till last night."

He was giving me the once-over. I knew what was going through his head. I knew the way a cop's mind worked like the back of my hand. A good cop's anyway. We'd had a few drinks, Sonia and I. We'd fucked. And then she'd sobered up, and decided to call it quits. It had been a mistake. She couldn't understand how it had happened. But it was the kind of thing that could happen to a single mother. A fatal mistake. Not uncommon. A mistake often made. Leading to a crime. And the fact that I was an ex-cop made no difference. You could still go crazy. You could still turn violent.

Unconsciously I suppose, I held out my hands towards him. "Nothing happened between us," I said. "Nothing at all. We were supposed to meet tonight, that's all."

"I'm not accusing you."

"I just wanted you to know."

Now it was my turn to give him the once-over. Béraud. A straight cop. Who'd liked working with a captain who was also straight.

"So the daycare center called you, is that it?"

"No. They started to get worried. She was always on time. Never late. So they called the boy's grandfather and . . ."

Attilio, I thought. Béraud paused. For me to take in what he was telling me. The grandfather, not the father. Clearly, he trusted me again.

"Not the father?" I said.

He shrugged. "They've never seen the father . . . The grandfather was upset. He'd already kept the boy last night, and was supposed to be keeping him tonight."

Béraud paused. And in that silence I thought of tonight, the night Sonia and I should have been spending together.

"She was supposed to feed him, give him his bath." He looked at me almost tenderly.

"So what happened?"

"He went to the daycare center to get the boy and take him home. Then he tried to contact his daughter at her office. But she'd left. At the same time as usual. So he called here. He thought that with it being as hot as it was, Sonia might have come home first to take a shower and . . . But there was no answer. That's when he started to get worried, and phoned her neighbor. Sonia and this neighbor often did favors for each other. When she came to the door, she found it half open. She was the one who called us."

The apartment filled with noise, voices.

Béraud stood up. "Hello, captain," he said.

I looked up. A tall young woman was standing there in front of me. In jeans and T-shirt, both black. An attractive woman. I extricated myself as best I could from the armchair I was sitting in.

"Is this the witness?" she asked.

"He used to be a cop. Fabio Montale."

She held out her hand. "Captain Pessayre."

She had a firm handshake. Her hand felt warm. Sharp black eyes, full of life and passion. For a fraction of a second, we stood looking at each other. Long enough to believe that the law could abolish death. And crime.

"Tell me all about it."

"I'm tired," I said, sitting down again. "Tired."

And my eyes filled with tears. At last.

Tears are the only cure for hate.

5.

IN WHICH EVEN SOMETHING POINTLESS
CAN BE GOOD TO SAY, AND GOOD TO HEAR

I hadn't spat at the stars. I couldn't.

Off the Riou Islands, I'd cut the motor and let the boat drift. It was here, more or less, that my father had held me under the armpits and dipped me in the sea for the first time. I was eight. The same age as Enzo. "Don't be afraid," he'd said. "Don't be afraid." It was the only baptism I'd ever had. And whenever life became too painful, this was where I came, here, between the sea and the sky. As if it was only here that I might be able to make peace with the world.

I'd come here when Lole left, too. I'd come to this spot and stayed here the whole night. One whole night running through all the things I blamed myself for. It had needed to be said. At least once. Even if it was just to the empty sky. It was December 16th. The cold chilled me to the bone. Even though I kept knocking back Lagavulin as I wept. Getting back home at dawn, I'd felt as if I was returning to the land of the dead.

I was alone now. In the silence. Wrapped in garlands of stars. Stars up above me in the blue-black sky, and below me, reflected on the surface of the sea. The only movement was the lapping of the water against my boat.

I stayed there for a long time, motionless, with my eyes closed. Until I felt the lump inside me, that mixture of disgust and sadness, start to dissolve. The cool air restored a human rhythm to my breathing. Liberating it from the anguish of living and dying.

Sonia.

"She's dead," I'd told them. "Murdered."

Fonfon and Honorine had been playing rummy on the terrace. Honorine's favourite card game. She always won, because she liked winning. Fonfon always let her win, because he liked to see her joy when she won. Fonfon had a *pastis* in front of him, Honorine what was left of her Martini. They'd looked up at me. Surprised to see me back so early. Worried, of course. And all I'd said was, "She's dead. Murdered."

I'd looked at them, then, a blanket and my jacket under my arm, and a bottle of Lagavulin in the other hand, I'd crossed the terrace, gone down the steps to the boat and set off into the darkness. Telling myself, as I always did, that this sea, which my father had offered me as a kingdom, would never belong to me, because I always used it to offload all the dirty tricks the world had played on me.

When I opened my eyes and saw the stars glimmering, I knew, once again, that this wasn't true. It was as if the world had stopped moving. Life was suspended. Except in my heart, where right now someone was crying. An eight-year-old boy and his grandfather.

I took a long swig of Lagavulin. Sonia's laughter, and then her voice, echoed in my head. Everything fell back into place. Clearly. Her laughter. Her voice. And her words.

"There's a place they call the *Eremo dannunziano*. It's a belvedere where Gabriele d'Annunzio often stayed . . ."

She'd started talking about Italy. About the Abruzzi, where her family came from. The stretch of coast between Ortona and Vasto which, according to her, "was unique in the world." Once she started she couldn't stop, and I'd listened, letting her pleasure flow into me as gladly as the glasses of *pastis* I was knocking back without a thought.

"The beach where I spent my summers when I was a kid is called Turchino. Turchino, because the water is turquoise. It's full of shingle and bamboo. You can make little junks out of the leaves, or fishing rods . . ."

I could see it all. And feel it. The water flowing over my skin. The gentleness of it. And the saltiness. The salty taste of bodies. Yes, I could see it all, so close I could touch it. Like Sonia's bare shoulder. As round, and as soft to the touch, as a pebble washed smooth by the sea. Sonia.

"There's a railway line all the way down to Foggia . . ."

She gazed fondly into my eyes. As if inviting me to take that train with her, and glide down to the sea. To Turchino.

"Life's so simple down there, Fabio. The rhythm of the train passing, the sound of the sea, pizza *al taglio* for lunch, and"—she added with a laugh—"*una gerla alla stracciatella per me* toward evening . . ."

Sonia.

There was laughter in her voice. Her words were full of the joys of life.

I hadn't been back to Italy since I was nine. My father had taken my mother and me to his village. Castel San Giorgio, near Salerno. He'd wanted to see his mother again, one last time. He'd wanted her to see me. I told Sonia about it. I told her how I'd thrown the worst tantrum of my life because I was pissed off eating pasta for lunch and dinner every day.

She laughed. "That's what I'd like to do now. Take my son to Italy. To Foggia. The way your father did with you."

She lifted her gray-blue eyes to me, slowly. It was like the dawn coming up. She was waiting for my reaction. A son. How could I have forgotten that she'd told me about her son? Enzo. I hadn't even remembered when the cops had questioned me. What was it I hadn't wanted to hear when she'd said "my son"?

I'd never wanted a child. With any woman. I was afraid I wouldn't know how to be a father. It wasn't that I couldn't give love, it was just that I didn't think I could teach a child trust—trust in the world, in me, in the future. I didn't see any future for the children of this century. Spending so many years in the police had a lot to do with it. It had distorted my vision of society. I'd seen more kids get into dope and petty crime, then graduate to bigger crimes and end up in jail, than succeed in life. Even those who liked school, who did well at it, eventually came to a dead end. And then they either banged their heads against the wall until they almost died, or they turned around, ready to fight back, to rebel against the injustice that was being done to them, and ended up in the same old cycle of violence, and guns. And jail.

The only woman I'd have liked to have a child with was Lole. But we'd told each other that we didn't want children. We were too old, that was our excuse. Often, though, when we were making love, I found myself hoping that she'd stopped taking the pill, without telling me. And that she'd announce one day, with a tender smile, "I'm expecting a baby, Fabio." A gift, for the two of us. For our love.

I knew I should have told her I felt that way. I also knew I should have told her I wanted to marry her, really wanted her to be my wife. She might have said no. But everything would have been clear between us. Whether the answer was yes or no, at least we would have talked about it, simply, like two people happy to be together. But I'd kept silent. And so had she, of course. Until the silence had torn us apart.

Instead of answering Sonia, I finished my drink.

"His father dumped me," she continued. "Five years ago. We've never heard from him since."

"That's tough," I heard myself saying.

She shrugged. "When a guy abandons his own son, never makes any attempt to contact him . . . Five years, you know, and not even at Christmas, not even on his birthday . . . Well, I guess it's better this way. He wouldn't have been a good father."

"But a child needs a father!"

Sonia had looked at me in silence. We were sweating

through every pore. Me more than her. Her thigh was still up against mine, lighting a fire I thought I'd never feel again. A raging inferno.

"I brought him up on my own. Well, my father helped, of course. Maybe one day I'll meet a guy I'll be happy to introduce to Enzo. He could never be his father, I know that, but I think he could give him what a child needs as it's growing up. Authority, and love. And trust. Dreams too. A man's dreams . . ."

Sonia.

At that moment, I had the impulse to put my arms around her and hold her. Gently, she freed herself, laughing. "Fabio."

"All right, all right." I raised my hands above my head, to show her I wouldn't touch her.

"We'll have a last drink, and then we'll go for a swim. O.K.?"

I'd thought to take her out in my boat. We'd go swimming in the sea. In deep water. In the very place I was right now. Thinking back on it, I was amazed I'd even suggested it. I'd only just met her. My boat was my desert island. My place to be alone. I'd only ever taken Lole out in it. The night she came to live with me. And Fonfon and Honorine, just recently. No other woman had ever been judged worthy to get in my boat. Not even Babette.

I'd signaled to Hassan to pour us another round. "Sure," he'd said.

Coltrane was playing. I was completely drunk, but I recognized "Out of This World." Fourteen minutes that could devour a whole night. Hassan would soon be closing, I realized. Coltrane was always to send his customers on their way. To their lovers. Or their lonely nights. Coltrane was for the road.

I was quite incapable of getting up from my chair.

"You're beautiful, Sonia."

"And you're plastered, Fabio."

We both roared with laughter.

Happiness. It was still possible.

Happiness.

The phone was ringing when I got in. Ten past two. Jerk, I said to whoever was daring to phone me at such an hour. I let it ring until they gave up.

Silence. I didn't feel tired. But I did feel hungry. Honorine had left a note for me in the kitchen. Propped up against the clay casserole she used for stews. "It's *soupe au pistou.* You can eat it cold if you like. Have some. Lots of love. Fonfon says hi." Next to it, in a little saucer, she'd put some grated cheese, just in case.

Soupe au pistou was vegetable soup with garlic and basil, and I suppose there were a thousand ways to make it. Everyone in Marseilles said, "My mother used to make it this way," and so that was how they made it. It always tasted different. It depended on the vegetables you put in. It depended especially on getting the garlic and the basil in the right proportions, and how you mixed both of them with tomato pulp heated in the same water you'd cooked the vegetables in.

Honorine made the best *soupe au pistou.* Haricot beans, kidney beans, French beans, a few potatoes and macaroni. She'd let it simmer all morning. Then she'd tackle the basil and garlic. Crushing them in an old wooden mortar. You really couldn't disturb her when she was doing that. "If you're going to stand there like a statue, watching me, I'll never finish."

I put the casserole on the stove, on a low flame. Vegetable soup with basil and garlic was even better when it had been reheated a couple of times. I lit a cigarette and poured some red wine from Bandol. A Tempier 91. My last bottle of the year. Maybe the best.

Had Sonia talked about all those things with Honorine? Or with Fonfon? About her life as a single mother. About Enzo. How had Sonia figured out I wasn't a happy man? She'd told Honorine that she thought I was "unhappy." I hadn't told her about Lole, I was sure of that. But I had talked about myself. I'd talked a lot about myself. About my life since I'd come back from Djibouti and become a cop.

Lole's departure was more than just something that made me unhappy, it was my great tragedy. But it may be that she had left because of my way of life. My attitude to life. I'd spent too long without really believing in life. Had I, without realizing it, become permanently unhappy? Believing as I did that the small joys of everyday life were enough to make you happy, had I given up on my dreams, my real dreams? And, at the same time, on the future? Whenever the dawn rose on a new day, as it was doing now, I never thought about tomorrow. I'd never gone to sea on a freighter. I'd never sailed to the other side of the world. I'd stayed here, in Marseilles. Loyal to a past that didn't exist anymore. To my parents. To my friends who were gone. And every time a friend died, it made me all the more reluctant to leave. I was trapped in this city. I'd never even gone back to Italy, to Castel San Giorgio . . .

Sonia. Maybe I'd have gone down there with her and Enzo, down to the Abruzzi. Maybe after that, I'd have taken her—or would she have had to urge me?—to Castel San Giorgio, so that both of them could fall in love with that beautiful region that was as much mine as this city where I was born.

I'd had a plateful of soup—lukewarm, the way I like it. Honorine had surpassed herself again. I finished the wine. I was ready to go to bed. To confront the nightmares. The images of death in my head. When I woke up, I'd go see Sonia's father. Attilio. And Enzo. "I'm the last man Sonia met," I'd say. "I'm not sure, but I think she liked me. And I liked her, too." It wouldn't make any difference, but there was no harm in saying it, and there couldn't be any harm in hearing it.

The phone started ringing again.

Angrily, I picked up the receiver. "Fuck!" I yelled, ready to hang up.

"Montale," the voice said.

That loathsome voice I'd heard twice the day before. Cold, in spite of the slight Italian accent.

"Montale," the voice repeated.

"Yeah."

"The girl, Sonia. That was just to make you realize we're not joking."

"What?" I cried.

"It's just the beginning, Montale. Just the beginning. You seem a little hard of hearing. A little stupid, too. So we'll carry on until you find the shit-stirrer for us. Do you hear me?"

"You bastards!" I screamed. Then, louder and louder, "You scumbag! You bastard! You piece of shit!"

Silence at the other end. But the guy hadn't hung up. He waited until I was out of breath, then said, "We're going to kill your friends, Montale. All of them. One by one. Until you find the Bellini woman. And if you don't shift your ass, by the time we've finished you're going to regret you're still alive. The choice is yours."

"O.K.," I said, feeling drained.

The faces of my friends flashed in front of my eyes. Ending with Fonfon and Honorine. *No*, my heart was weeping. *No.*

"O.K.," I repeated, in a low voice.

"We'll call again tonight." He hung up.

"I'm going to kill you, you bastard!" I screamed. "I'm going to kill you! I'm going to kill you!"

I turned, and saw Honorine. She'd put on the dressing gown I'd given her for Christmas. Her hands were folded over her stomach, and she was looking at me in terror.

"I thought you were having a nightmare. You were screaming."

"The only nightmares are when you're awake," I said.

My hate had returned. And with it, that stench of death.

I knew I'd have to kill the guy.

6.

IN WHICH THE LOVE WE SHARE WITH A CITY IS OFTEN A SECRET LOVE

The phone was ringing. Nine-ten. Shit! The phone had never before rung so much in my house. I lifted the receiver, expecting the worst. Just doing that made me break out in a sweat. It was getting hotter and hotter. Even with the windows open, there wasn't the slightest breath of air.

"Yeah?" I said grouchily.

"Captain Pessayre. Good morning. Are you always in such a bad mood in the mornings?"

I loved that low, slightly drawling voice.

"In case someone's trying to sell me a fitted kitchen!"

She laughed. There was something gravelly about her laugh. I guessed she was from the Southwest, that neck of the woods.

"Can I see you this morning?"

It was the same warm voice. But it was clear she wouldn't take no for an answer. We'd definitely be meeting this morning.

"Something wrong?"

"Oh, no . . . We looked into your statement. Your movements check out. Don't worry, you're not a suspect."

"Thanks."

"I've . . . Let's just say I'd like to talk to you about a few things."

"Ah!" I said, falsely cheerful. "If it's an invitation, there's no problem."

This time she didn't laugh. And I found it reassuring that she wasn't taken in by me. This was a woman with a strong character and, as I didn't know how things were going to turn out, it was better to know who I could count on. Among the cops, obviously.

"Eleven o'clock."

"In your office?"

"I don't suppose you're too crazy about that idea."

"Not really."

"How about the Fort Saint-Jean? We can go for a little walk, if you like."

"I like it over there."

"Me too."

I'd driven in along the Corniche. I didn't want to lose sight of the sea. There are days like that. When I can't enter downtown Marseilles any other way. When I need the city to come to me. I'm the one moving, but it's the city that comes closer. If I could, I'd always come to Marseilles by sea. Once past the Malmousque cove, the harbor entrance always moved me deeply. I was Edouard Peisson's sailor, Hans. Or Blaise Cendrars, coming back from Panama. Or Rimbaud, "a fresh angel who landed in the port yesterday morning." It was a constant replay of the moment when Protis, the Phocean, entered the harbor, his eyes wide with wonder.

The city was transparent this morning. Pink and blue in the still air. Hot already, but not yet sticky. Marseilles was inhaling its own light. As carefree as the customers on the terrace of La Samaritaine, drinking it down to the last drop of coffee in their cups. The roofs were blue, the sea pink. Or vice versa. Until noon. After that, for a few hours, the sun would crush everything. The shade as well as the light. The city would turn opaque. White. And the whole of Marseilles would smell of anise.

In fact, I was starting to feel thirsty. I'd have liked a nice cool *pastis*, on a shady terrace. At Ange's, for example, on

Place des Treize-Coins, in my old neighborhood, the Panier. My hangout in the days when I was a cop.

"That's where I learned to swim," I said to her, pointing to the harbor entrance.

She smiled. She had just joined me at the foot of the Fort Saint-Jean. Striding up to me with a cigarette in her mouth. She was wearing jeans and a T-shirt, like the day before. They were off-white this time. Her auburn hair was drawn back behind her neck in a little bun. Deep in her dark hazel eyes, there was a wicked gleam. She could easily pass for about thirty. But she must be at least ten years older.

I pointed to the other shore. "You had to swim across and then back if you wanted to show you were a man. And have any chance of making out with girls."

She smiled again. Revealing, this time, two pretty dimples in her cheeks.

In front of us, three elderly couples with weatherbeaten skin were getting ready to dive into the water. They were regulars. This was where they bathed, not on the beach. Out of loyalty to their own youth, I supposed. For a long time, Ugo, Manu and I had continued coming here to swim. Lole, who rarely bathed, would come and join us, bringing a snack. We'd lie on the flat stones and dry off listening to her reading her favourite lines from *Exile* by Saint-John Perse.

> . . . *we'll head more than one cortege, singing yesterday, singing elsewhere, singing evil at its birth*
> *And the splendor of life going into exile interminably this year.*

The elderly people dived into the water—the women wearing white caps—and swam toward the Pharo cove, with confident, skillful strokes. They weren't showing off. They didn't have to impress anyone anymore. They impressed themselves.

I watched them as they swam. I was willing to bet they'd all met here when they were sixteen or seventeen. Six friends, three men and three women. And now they were growing old together. Enjoying the simple pleasure of feeling the sun on their skin. That was what life here was all about. Loyalty to the simplest actions.

"Is that what you like, making out with girls?"

"I'm past all that," I replied, as seriously as possible.

"Oh, right," she replied, just as seriously. "That's hard to believe."

"If you're talking about Sonia . . ."

"No. I'm talking about the way you look at me. Not many men are so direct."

"I have a weakness for beautiful women."

She burst out laughing. The same laugh she'd had on the phone. A frank laugh, like water flowing from a hollow. Harsh but warm. "I'm not what people call a beautiful woman."

"All women say that, until a man seduces them."

"You seem to know a lot about it."

I was disoriented by the turn the conversation was taking. What the hell are you saying? I asked myself. She looked hard at me, and I felt awkward suddenly. She certainly knew how to get people to talk.

"I know a little," I said. "Shall we walk, captain?"

"Call me Hélène. Yes, I'd like that."

We walked alongside the sea until we reached the outer harbor of La Joliette. Facing the Sainte-Marie lighthouse. Like me, she loved this spot, from where you could see the ferries and the freighters going in and out. And like me, she was worried by all the plans for the port. There was one word on the lips of the politicians and the technocrats. Euroméditerranée. Everyone, even those who'd been born here, like the current mayor, was looking toward Europe. Northern Europe, of course. Capital: Brussels.

The only future for Marseilles lay in rejecting its own history. That's what we were being told. All this talk about redeveloping the port was a way of saying that we had to finish with the port as it was today—the symbol of a bygone glory. Even the Marseilles longshoremen, tough as they were, had come around in the end.

So the hangars would be razed to the ground. J3. J4. The quays would be redesigned. Tunnels would be bored. Expressways would be created. Esplanades. The street layout and the housing provision would be rethought, from Place de la Joliette all the way to the Saint-Charles station. And the maritime landscape would be restructured. That was the great new idea. The great new priority. The maritime landscape.

The things you read in the newspapers were enough to leave any citizen of Marseilles bewildered. Of the hundred berths in the four harbor basins, it was said that they somehow worked "as if by magic." To the technocrats, that meant chaos. Let's be realistic, they said, let's put an end to this charming, nostalgic, but obsolete landscape. I'd laughed out loud one day, reading in *Marseilles*—a serious magazine—that the history of the city "through its exchanges with the outside world will find in its own social and economic roots the inspiration for a new, nobler downtown area."

"Here, read this," I'd said to Fonfon.

"Why do you buy that crap?" he'd asked, giving me back the magazine.

"Because there's a special report on the Panier. That's our history."

"We don't have a history anymore, my friend. What remains of it they're planning to shove up our asses. And I'm being polite."

"Taste this."

I'd poured some white Tempier into his glass. It was eight o'clock. We were on the terrace of his bar. With four dozen sea urchins in front of us.

"Hey!" he said, clicking his tongue. "Where did you get this?"

"I have two crates. Six '91 reds. Six '92 reds. Six '95 rosés and six '95 whites."

I'd become friendly with Lulu, the owner of the estate, in the Plan du Castellet. She and I would taste the wines and talk about literature. Poetry. There were poems by Louis Brauquier she knew by heart. From *Harbor Bar*. And *Freedom of the Seas*.

> *I am still far and can afford to be brave*
> *But the day will come when we are beneath your wind . . .*

Had those technocrats from Paris and their landscape architects ever read Brauquier? Or Gabriel Audisio? Or Toursky? Or Gérald Neveu? Did they know that in 1925, a man named Jean Ballard, who worked in a weigh-house, had created the finest literary magazine of the century, *Les Cahiers du Sud*, which did more than all the trading in goods to spread the glory of Marseilles on all the boats in all the ports in the world?

"Going back to the bullshit in that magazine," Fonfon had said, "I'll tell you this. When they start talking about a noble downtown area, you know what that means? Everybody out. A clean sweep! The Arabs, the Comorians, the blacks. Anyone who doesn't fit. The unemployed, the poor . . . Out they go!"

Or, as my old friend Mavros, who scraped a living from his boxing gym up in Saint-Antoine, used to say, "Any time someone talks to you about nobility, trust, honor, just look over your shoulder and you're almost sure to find someone about to shove his dick up your ass." I couldn't quite accept that, and Mavros and I always ended up arguing.

"You're exaggerating, Fonfon."

"Oh, sure. Go on, pour me another drink. That'll stop you talking crap."

Hélène Pessayre had the same fears about the future of Marseilles as a port. "You know," she said, "the South, the Mediterranean . . . We're always out of luck. We belong to what the technocrats call the 'dangerous classes' of the future." She opened her bag and took out a book. "Have you read this?"

The book was *Faith and Credit: The World Bank's Secular Empire* by Susan George and Fabrizio Sabelli.

"Interesting?"

"Fascinating. According to this book, now that the Cold War is over and the West is trying to assimilate the Eastern bloc—mostly to the detriment of the Third World—the myth of the dangerous classes has been revived, but now it refers to the South, to migrants from the South to the North."

We'd sat down on a stone bench. Next to an old Arab who lay there with a smile on his face, apparently asleep. Down below, sitting on the rocks, two anglers, both unemployed or on welfare I guessed, were checking their lines.

In front of us, the open sea. The infinite blueness of the world.

"To those in Northern Europe, the South is by its very nature chaotic, radically different, and therefore disturbing. I think I agree with the authors of this book: the countries of the North will end up building a new frontier, what the Romans used to call a *limes*, to protect them from the barbarians."

I whistled through my teeth. I was sure Fonfon and Mavros would like this woman.

"We're going to pay the price for this new vision of the

world. By 'we' I mean the poor, the unemployed, and all the kids too, the ones from North Marseilles you see hanging around town."

"And I thought I was a pessimist," I said with a laugh.

"Pessimism doesn't get you anywhere, Montale. This new world is a closed world. Finite, ordered, stable. There's no place in it for the likes of us. A new philosophy holds sway. Judeo-Christian, Hellenistic, democratic. With its myth of the new barbarians. Us. And we're uncountable, undisciplined, nomads of course. We're also uncontrollable, fanatical, violent. And poor, of course. Reason and law are on the other side of the frontier. Wealth too."

Her eyes were veiled with sadness. She shrugged her shoulders and stood up. Her hands thrust deep in the pockets of her jeans, she walked to the edge of the water and stood there, silent, staring out toward the horizon. I joined her. She pointed to the open sea.

"That's the way I came to Marseilles for the first time. By sea. I was six years old. I've never forgotten how beautiful the city was early in the morning. I've never forgotten Algiers either. But I've never been back. Do you know Algiers?"

"No. I haven't done much traveling."

"I was born there. I fought for years to be transferred here, to Marseilles. Marseilles isn't Algiers. But from here, it's as if I can see the harbor over there. I also learned to swim by jumping off the docks into the water. To impress the boys. We'd swim out to the buoys, on the open sea. The boys would follow us out and swim around us, shouting, 'Hey, did you see the pretty seagull!' We were all pretty seagulls."

She turned to look at me, her eyes shining with past happiness.

"The love we share with a city . . ." I began.

"Is often a secret love," she finished the phrase, with a smile. "I like Camus too."

I offered her a cigarette, and lit it for her. She breathed in the smoke, threw her head back and slowly blew the smoke into the air. Then she gave me a long, steady look. Maybe now I'd finally find out why she'd wanted to meet me this morning.

"You didn't ask me here just to talk about all this, did you?"

"You're right, Montale. I'd like you to talk me about the Mafia!"

"The Mafia!"

She gave me a piercing look. Hélène was Captain Pessayre again. "How about a drink?" she said.

7.

IN WHICH THERE ARE SOME MISTAKES
TOO TERRIBLE FOR REMORSE

Ange embraced me. "Dammit, I didn't think I'd ever see you again!" Then, seeing Hélène sitting down on the terrace, beneath the magnificent plane trees, he winked at me. "That's one hell of an attractive woman!"

"She's a police captain."

"No!"

"She is, I tell you." I laughed. "You see, I'm bringing you a new kind of customer."

"You're dumb, you know that?"

Hélène ordered a *mauresque*, I ordered a *pastis*.

"Are you eating here?" Ange asked.

I gave Hélène a questioning look. Maybe what she wanted to ask me didn't leave any room for Ange's simple, but always delicious, dish of the day.

"I have some small mullet," he suggested. "They're wonderful grilled, with a little *bohémienne* sauce. And as a starter, there's a *feuilleté* of sardines—fresh sardines, of course. The best thing in this heat is fish."

"I agree," she said.

"Do you still have that Puy-Sainte-Réparade rosé?"

"Sure! I'll bring you a carafe to start."

We clinked glasses. I felt as if I'd known this woman forever. We'd formed an immediate bond. Ever since we shook hands the night before. Our conversation by the sea had merely confirmed it.

I didn't know what was happening to me. But in forty-eight hours, two very different women had managed to get inside me. I guess I'd been steering clear of women, and of love, since Lole had left. Sonia had opened the door of my heart and now anyone who wanted could come in. Well, not just anyone. I was sure Hélène Pessayre wasn't just anyone.

"O.K., I'm listening," I said.

"I've been reading about you. At the office. Official reports. You've twice been involved in cases with Mafia connections. The first time after your friend Ugo died, part of the war between Zucca and Batisti. The second time when a hitman named Narni came to Marseilles to settle a few scores."

"And killed a sixteen-year-old boy. Yes, I know. Coincidence. What of it?"

"If it happened twice, it can happen three times, can't it?"

"I don't follow you," I said, trying not to seem too dumb.

I followed her only too well. And I wondered how she'd managed to come up with this theory so quickly.

She gave me quite a severe look. "You like to play the fool, is that it, Montale?"

"What makes you think that? Just because I don't know what you're talking about?"

"Sonia's death wasn't a random killing, Montale. Some maniac with a knife who just happened to break into her apartment."

"Maybe it was her husband," I said, as innocently as I could. "I mean, the boy's father."

"Sure, sure . . ." She tried to look in my eyes, but I kept them trained on my glass.

I emptied it in one go, trying to appear composed. "Another *mauresque*?"

"No, thanks."

"Ange!" I called. "Give me another *pastis*."

As soon as the drink had been poured, she said, "I see you haven't gotten out of the habit of telling tall stories."

"Listen, Hélène—"

"Captain. These are a captain's questions. Part of a criminal investigation. An investigation into the death of a woman named Sonia De Luca, the mother of an eight-year-old boy. Unmarried. Thirty-four years old. Thirty-four, Montale. The same age as me." Imperceptibly, she'd raised her voice.

"I know that. This was a woman who won me over in a single night. And then she talked to my two dearest neighbors for five minutes and won them over, too. She was a wonderful woman, no doubt about it."

"And what else do you know?"

"Nothing!"

"That's bullshit!" she cried.

Ange served us the sardine *feuilleté*. He looked from one to the other. "Enjoy," he said.

"Thanks."

"Hey! If he bothers you, you just call me."

She smiled.

I echoed Ange. "Enjoy."

"I will." She swallowed a mouthful, then put down her knife and fork. "Montale, I spent a long time on the phone with Loubet this morning. Before I called you."

"Oh, yes. How's he doing?"

"As well as you'd expect for someone who's been given the push. As I'm sure you can imagine. He says he'd like to hear from you."

"Right. I should have done it before. I'll call him. So what did he tell you about me?"

"That you're a pain in the ass. A good man, an honest man, but a royal pain in the ass. Capable of withholding information from the police, just to give yourself a head start and settle things your own way. Like a grown-up."

"Loubet's just flattering me."

"And when you finally deigned to let go, things were always in a worse mess than before."

"Oh, sure!" I said, irritably.

Loubet was right, of course. But I was stubborn. And I didn't trust the cops anymore. The racists, the officers on the take. The ones whose only concern was climbing the career ladder. Loubet was an exception. In every town, cops like him could be counted on the fingers of both hands. The exception that proved the rule. Our police really believed in liberty, equality and fraternity.

I looked Hélène in the eyes. The wicked gleam had gone, so had the nostalgia for past happiness. And so had that feminine softness I'd caught glimpses of.

"I don't care," I said. "The corpses, the blunders, the mistakes, the harassment, the beatings . . . That's always you people. I don't have blood on my hands!"

"Neither do I, Montale. And neither does Loubet, as far as I know! Stop with that! What are you trying to do? Play Superman? Get yourself killed?"

I remembered some terrible murders committed by Mafia hitmen. One of them named Giovanni Brusca had strangled an eleven-year-old boy with his bare hands. The son of Santino di Matteo, a veteran of the Corleone family who'd turned State's evidence. Brusca had then thrown the boy's body in an acid bath. Sonia's killer must be a graduate of the same school.

"Maybe," I muttered. "Would that bother you?"

"Yes, it would."

She bit her lower lip. The words had slipped out. They gave me a brief tingle of excitement, then I quickly forgot them, and told myself I might have a chance to regain the upper hand in this conversation. She might be a captain, but I had absolutely no intention of talking to Hélène Pessayre about the Mafia. About the one-in-a-million chance that had cost Sonia her life. Or about the killer's phone calls. Much less about Babette being on the run. At least, for the moment, as far as Babette was concerned.

No, they couldn't change me. I'd do what I always did. What I felt was right. And ever since that bastard had phoned, I'd been seeing things very simply. I'd arrange to meet with the guy, the killer, and empty my gun into his belly. I'd take him by surprise. He'd never imagine that an idiot like me could handle a gun, let alone kill him. Hitmen all think they're better, more cunning than anyone else. They think they stand out from the crowd. It wouldn't change anything about the mess Babette had gotten herself into. But it would relieve some of the grief in my heart.

I'd left home yesterday afternoon, certain I was going to bring Sonia back with me. We'd have had breakfast on my terrace, we'd have gone swimming in the sea, and Honorine would have come over and suggested what to eat for lunch and dinner. And in the evening all four of us would have had dinner together.

An idyllic vision. That was what I always did with reality. Tried to raise it to the level of my dreams. To the level of a man's eyes. The level of happiness. But reality was like a reed. It bent, but it didn't break. Behind the illusion, you could never lose sight of human corruption. Or death. Death, which has eyes for everyone.

I'd never killed anyone. But now I thought I could do it. I could kill. And I could die. Killing meant dying, too. I had nothing left to lose. I'd lost Lole. I'd lost Sonia. Two chances of happiness. One I knew about. The other I'd only glimpsed. They were identical. All loves take the same road, and reinvent it. Lole had been able to reinvent our love in another love. I could have reinvented Lole with Sonia. Maybe.

It didn't matter anymore.

I thought of a poem by Cesare Pavese called "Death Will Come and Will Have Your Eyes."

The eyes of love.

It will be like giving up a vice,
Like seeing a dead face
Appear in the mirror,
Like listening to closed lips.
We will descend silently into the whirlpool.

Of course, Fonfon and Honorine wouldn't forgive me for dying. But they'd both survive. Their lives had been based on love. Tenderness. Loyalty. That was how they'd lived, and they'd continue living like that. Their lives weren't failures. Unlike mine . . . "When you come down to it," I told myself, "the only way to give death a meaning is to feel gratitude for everything that went before."

And I had gratitude to spare.

"Montale." Her voice was soft now. "Sonia was killed by a professional hitman."

Hélène Pessayre had finally gotten around to telling me what she'd been wanting to tell me.

"The killer left a signature. Only the Mafia cuts people's throats that way. From right to left."

"How do you know about things like that?" I said, wearily.

The mullet arrived, and brought something of real life back to our table.

"Delicious," she said, after the first mouthful. "I do know about things like that. I did my law thesis on the Mafia. It's an obsession of mine."

I almost told her about Babette. She, too, was completely obsessed with the Mafia. I could have asked Hélène Pessayre what was behind this obsession. I'd have liked to know what it was that had driven her to waste her youth dissecting the machinery of the Mafia. It might have helped me to understand how Babette had gotten so caught up in that machinery that her life was in danger. Hers and quite a few others. I didn't do it. What I suspected horrified me. The fascination with death. With crime. Organized crime. Instead, I got angry.

"Who are you? Where have you been? Where do you think these questions and hypotheses are going to get you? Huh? To the back of a broom closet, like Loubet?"

A muted rage was rising inside me. The kind I always felt when I thought about the world's corruption.

"Don't you have anything else to do with your life? Just dealing with all this shit? Wearing out your lovely eyes on bloodstained corpses? Huh? Don't you have a husband to keep you at home? Don't you have a kid to raise? Is that your life, being able to recognize that one throat has been cut by the Mafia and another one by a sex maniac? Is that it?"

"Yes, that's my life. Just that, nothing else."

She placed her hand on mine. As if I were her lover. As if she were about to say, "I love you."

No, I couldn't tell her what I knew, not yet. I had to find Babette first. It was as if I was setting myself a time limit during which it was all right to lie. I'd find Babette, I'd talk to her, and only then would I give Hélène Pessayre the whole story, not before. No, before that, I'd kill the guy. The son of a bitch who'd killed Sonia.

Hélène's eyes searched mine. She was an amazing woman. But she was starting to scare me. Because of what she was capable of getting me to say. Because of what she was capable of doing too.

She didn't say, "I love you." What she said was, "Loubet's right."

"What else did he say about me?"

"That you're sensitive. Over sensitive. You're an incurable romantic, Montale."

She took her hand away from mine, leaving me with a real feeling of emptiness. There was an abyss between us. Her hand was far from mine now, and it made me feel dizzy. I was about to plunge in. And tell her everything.

No, I'd kill the fucking hitman first.

"Well?" she asked.

Yes, before anything else, I had to kill him.

Empty my hate into his belly.

Sonia.

And all that hate inside me. Hardening inside my body.

"Well what?" I replied, as laconically as I could.

"Are you in trouble with the Mafia?"

"When's Sonia's funeral?"

"When I sign the burial certificate."

"And when are you planning to do that?"

"When you've answered my question."

"No!"

"Yes."

We looked straight at each other. Violence against violence. Truth against truth. Justice against justice. But I had an advantage over her. The hate I was feeling. For the first time. I didn't flinch.

"I can't give you an answer. I have plenty of enemies. In North Marseilles. In the joint. Among the cops. And in the Mafia."

"A pity, Montale."

"What is?"

"You know, there are some mistakes so terrible, you can't even feel remorse."

"Why should I feel remorse?"

"Maybe it was your fault Sonia died."

My heart jumped. As if it wanted to escape, to leave my body, to fly away. To go somewhere where there was peace. If such a place existed. Hélène Pessayre had hit me right where it hurt the most. Because that was precisely what I'd been brooding over. Thanks to me, thanks to the fact that she'd been attracted to me the other night, Sonia had ended up at the end of a killer's knife. I'd only just met her, and they'd killed her to make it clear to me they weren't joking. The first on their list. In their cold logic, there were degrees of closeness, like the rungs on a ladder. Sonia was at the bottom of the ladder. Honorine right at the top, with Fonfon one rung below her.

I had to find Babette. As quickly as possible. Though I'd have to reason with myself to stop from strangling her as soon as I saw her.

Hélène Pessayre stood up. "She was the same age as me, Montale. I won't forgive you."

"For what?"

"For lying to me, if you have."

I had lied to her. Was I going to keep lying?

She was leaving. Striding to the counter with her coin purse in her hand, to pay for her meal. I'd stood up. Ange was looking at me, without really understanding.

"Hélène."

She turned. As quickly as a teenager. And for a fraction of a second, I had a glimpse of the young girl she must have been in Algiers. Summer in Algiers. A pretty seagull. Proud. Free. I also had a glimpse of her tanned young body, and the outline of her muscles as she dived into the water of the harbor. And the men looking at her.

The way I was looking at her now. Twenty years later.

I didn't know what to say. I stood there, looking at her.

"See you around," I said.

"Maybe," she said, sadly. "Bye."

8.

IN WHICH WHAT YOU CAN UNDERSTAND YOU CAN ALSO FORGIVE

Georges Mavros was waiting for me. He was the only friend I still had. The last one of my generation. Ugo and Manu were dead. The others had gone off to different places. Places where they'd found work. Where they were able to make a go of things. Where they'd met women. Most of them to Paris. Every now and again, one of them would give me a ring. To tell me how he was doing. To tell me he and his family were in town, between trains, or planes, or boats. There'd be time for a quick lunch or dinner. Marseilles was just a place of transit to them now. A stopover. But over the years the calls had become much less frequent. Life swallowed friendship. Some lost their jobs, or their marriages broke up. Not to mention those I'd erased from my memory, and from my address book, because they sympathized with the National Front.

Once you get to a certain age, you don't make friends anymore. But you still have buddies. People you hang out with, party with, play cards or bowls with. The years passed like that. With them. Between one person's birthday and another. Evenings spent eating and drinking. Dancing. The children grew up. They'd bring along their gorgeous girlfriends, who'd seduce their fathers and the friends of their friends, playing with their desire, as only girls between fifteen and eighteen can do. The couples would drink and gossip about each other's infidelities. And you also saw couples falling apart within the space of a single evening.

Mavros lost Pascale during one of those evenings. It was three years ago, the end of summer, at Marie and Pierre's place. They had a beautiful house in Malmousque, on Rue de la Douane, and they loved having friends over. I was very fond of Marie and Pierre.

Lole and I had been dancing salsa. Juan Luis Guerra, Arturo Sandoval, Irakere, Tito Puente, and to finish, Ray Barretto's magnificent "Benedicion." We were out of breath, our bodies fairly aroused after clinging to each other for so long.

Mavros was standing alone, leaning awkwardly against a wall, a glass of champagne in his hand.

"Are you O.K.?" I asked him.

He raised his glass, as if in a toast, and knocked back the drink. "Absolutely fine."

And he went off to get another drink. He was clearly determined to get plastered. I watched him as he went. Pascale, his girlfriend of five years, was at the other end of the room, deep in conversation with her old friend Joëlle and Benoît, a Marseilles photographer we occasionally met at parties. From time to time, someone would pass, join in their conversation, and walk off again.

I stood there for a moment watching the three of them. Pascale was in profile. She was monopolizing the conversation, talking nineteen to the dozen the way she sometimes did when she was passionate about something, or someone. Benoît had moved closer to her. So close, he seemed to be leaning his shoulder on hers. From time to time, he'd place his hand on the back of a chair, and Pascale would push back her long hair and then bring down her hand so that it rested next to his, but without touching it. It was mutual seduction, that much was obvious. And I wondered if Joëlle realized what was happening right there in front of her eyes.

Mavros was dying to join them, but he stayed where he was, drinking alone. With a kind of desperate determination. At one point, Pascale left Joëlle and Benoît, I assumed to go to the toilet, and walked right past him without saying a word. On the way back, she noticed him at last, went up to him, smiled, and asked, very gently, "Are you all right?"

"I don't exist anymore, is that it?" he replied.

"Why do you say that?"

"I've been watching you for an hour, I've been pouring myself drinks right next to you. You haven't looked at me once. It's as if I didn't exist. Is that it?"

Pascale didn't answer. She turned around and went back to the toilet. To cry. Because it was true. He didn't exist for her anymore. In her heart. But she hadn't yet admitted it to herself. Until she heard Mavros come right out with it.

One night a month later, Pascale stayed out all night. Mavros was in Limoges, sorting out the details of a fight he was arranging for one of his protégés. He phoned Pascale almost every hour during the night. He started to get worried. He was afraid something had happened to her—she'd had an accident, she'd been attacked. He kept leaving messages for her. The next day, Pascale left him one: *Nothing's happened to me. I'm not in hospital. I'm all right. I didn't go home last night. I'm at the office. Call me if you want to.*

After Pascale had left, Mavros and I spent a few nights together. Drinking, talking about the past, about life, love, women. Mavros felt wretched, and I couldn't do anything to help him regain his self-confidence.

Now he was living alone.

"You know, I used to wake up at night sometimes, and there'd be light coming through the shutters, and I'd just lie there for hours watching Pascale sleeping. She'd often be lying on her side, with her face turned to me, and a hand under her cheek. And I'd say to myself, 'She's more beautiful than ever. Gentler.' Her face at night made me happy, Fabio."

Lole's face had made me happy, too. I loved the mornings best of all. Waking up. Kissing her on the forehead, stroking her cheek, her neck. Until she stretched out her arm and put her hand on the back of my neck and pulled me to her to kiss me. It was always a good day for love.

"One separation is like another, Georges," I'd said to him when he'd called me after Lole left. "Everyone suffers. Everyone feels pain."

Mavros had been the only one to phone me. He was a real friend. That day, I'd made a complete break with all the buddies. And their parties. I should have done it before. Because they'd dropped Mavros. Gradually the invitations had dried up. They all liked Pascal and Benoît. And they all preferred happy relationships. It made life easier for them. It also stopped them from thinking the same thing could happen to them one day.

"Yeah," he'd replied. "Except that if you love someone else, you have a shoulder to lay your head on, a hand to stroke your cheek, and . . . You see, Fabio, the new desire takes away the pain of the old one."

"I don't know about that."

"I do."

The pain of Pascale's leaving was still with him. As Lole's was with me. But I was trying to find a meaning in what Lole had decided to do. Because it had to have a meaning. Lole hadn't left me for no reason. By now, I'd finally understood a lot of things, and what I could understand I could forgive.

"How's about we spar a little?"

The boxing gym hadn't changed. It was as clean as ever. Only the posters on the walls had turned yellow. But Mavros was attached to his posters. They were a reminder that he'd been a good boxer. And a good trainer. These days, he didn't arrange matches. He gave lessons. To the neighborhood kids. And the local town council gave him a small grant to keep his gym in good condition. Everyone in the neighborhood agreed it was better to see the kids learning to box than setting fire to cars or smashing store windows.

"You smoke too much, Fabio," he said. He hit me in the abdominals. "You're a little flabby here."

"How about here?" I said, hitting him on the chin.

"Yeah, me too!" He laughed. "Come on, let's see what you can do."

Mavros and I had fought over a girl in this ring. We were sixteen. Her name was Ophelia. We were both in love with her. But we were good friends, and we didn't want to fall out over a girl.

"Whoever wins on points," he'd suggested. "Three rounds."

His father, who found the whole thing amusing, agreed to referee. He was the one who'd started the gym, with the help of a sporting and cultural association connected to the CGT.

Mavros was a whole lot better than me. In the third round, he drew me into a corner of the ring, clinging to me, and started hitting me hard. But I was angrier than him. I wanted Ophelia. As he hit me, I caught my breath, freed myself, and got him back into the middle of the ring. There, I managed to land about twenty blows. I could hear him breathing against my shoulder. We were both as strong as each other. My desire for Ophelia compensated for my lack of technique. Just before the bell, I hit him on the nose. Mavros lost his balance and tried to support himself on the ropes. I kept punching, though I was at the point of exhaustion. A few seconds more, and he might have laid me out with a single uppercut.

His father declared me the winner. Mavros and I embraced. But come Friday night, Ophelia decided she wanted to go out with him. Not me.

Mavros had married her. She had just turned twenty. He was twenty-one, with a good career as a middleweight ahead of him. But she had forced him to give up boxing, which she couldn't stand. He'd become a truck driver, until one day he realized she was cheating on him every time he went out on the road.

Twenty minutes later, I threw in the sponge. I was out of breath, and my arms felt weak. I spat out my mouth guard into my glove and went and sat down on the bench. I was too exhausted to keep my head up straight, and let it drop between my shoulders.

"So, champion, giving up?"

"Go to hell!" I hissed.

He burst out laughing. "Let's take a shower, and then we'll go get a cold beer."

That was exactly what I had in mind. A shower and a beer.

Less than an hour later, we were sitting on the terrace of the Bar des Minimes, on Chemin Saint-Antoine. By the time we were on our second beers, I'd told Mavros everything that had happened. From the time I met Sonia to my lunch with Hélène Pessayre.

"I have to find Babette."

"Yeah, and what are you going to do then? Have her giftwrapped and hand her over to those guys?"

"I don't know, Georges. But I have to find her. I need to know just how serious this is. Maybe we can come to some kind of arrangement with them."

"Are you kidding? You think guys who'd kill a girl just to get you up off your ass are the kind of guys you can talk to?"

The fact was, I didn't know. I couldn't think straight. Sonia's death was elbowing out every other thought in my head. But one thing was for sure: I might have been angry with Babette for triggering this horror, but I couldn't see myself handing her over to the Mafia. I didn't want her killed.

"You may be on their list," I said, jokily.

The possibility had only just crossed my mind, and it sent a shiver down my spine.

"I don't think so. If they whack too many of the people around you, the cops won't let you out of their sight. And then you won't be able to do what these guys are expecting of you."

That made sense. After all, how could they know Mavros was a friend of mine? I went to his gym to work out, the same way I went to Hassan's bar to drink. Were they going to kill Hassan, too? No, Mavros was right.

"You're right," I said.

His eyes, though, told me it's easier to say things than to believe them. Not that Mavros was afraid. But there was anxiety in his eyes. It was understandable. We weren't afraid of death, but we'd have preferred it to strike us later rather than sooner, and if possible in bed, after a good night's sleep.

"You know, Georges, whatever coaching you're doing, you could put off till later. Why don't you take a vacation? It's a good time for it. A few days chilling out in the mountains . . . A week at the most."

"I don't have anywhere to chill out. And I don't want to. I've told you how I see things, Fabio. What if they come after you? Beat you up? I don't want to be too far from here if that happens. O.K.?"

"O.K. But keep your distance. This is nothing to do with you. Babette is my concern. You hardly know her."

"I know her well enough. And she's a friend of yours."

He looked at me. His eyes had changed. They had turned coal black, but without the brightness of anthracite. There was nothing in them but a great tiredness.

"The way I look at it," he said, "what have we got to lose? We've been screwed all our fucking lives. Our women have dumped us. We never had kids. So what's left? Friendship."

"That's why I don't want to throw it away. I don't want to serve it up on a plate to those vultures."

"O.K., pal," he said, patting me on the shoulder. "One

more drink, and I'll be on my way. I have a date with a stationmaster's wife."

"Really!"

He laughed. This was the Mavros I'd known in my teens. A fighter, big, strong, self-confident. And a ladies' man.

"No, she works in the post office next door. She's from Réunion. Her husband walked out on her and her two kids. I play at being daddy in the evening, it keeps me occupied."

"And later you play with the mommy."

"Hey," he said, "we're not too old for it yet, are we?" He finished his drink. "She doesn't expect anything from me, and I don't expect anything from her. But we make the nights less long for each other."

I got back to my car and put on a Pinetop Perkins cassette. *After Hours.* To take me back downtown.

Marseilles blues was still my style.

I made a detour along the coast. On those metal bridges the consultant landscape architects of Euroméditerrannée wanted to destroy. In that article in the magazine *Marseilles*, they called them "a cold, repellent universe of machines, concrete and rivets under the sun." The idiots!

From here, the harbor looked magnificent. You got a real eyeful of it as you drove. The piers. The freighters. The cranes. The ferries. The sea. The Château d'If and the islands of the Frioul in the distance. All ready for the taking.

9.

IN WHICH WE LEARN THAT
IT'S HARD TO SURVIVE THE DEAD

We were driving fender to fender. A lot of people were hooting their horns. From the Corniche onward, there'd been nothing but long lines of cars in both directions. Everyone in Marseilles seemed to be on the terraces of the ice cream parlors and bars and restaurants along the seafront. At the rate we were going, I'd soon be running out of cassettes. I'd followed Pinetop Perkins with Lightnin' Hopkins. *Darling, Do You Remember Me?*

Things were starting to stir in my head. Memories. For months now, my thoughts had been slipping away from me. I found it hard to focus on any one thing, even fishing—and that really was serious. The more time passed, the more important Lole's absence came to seem. It dominated my life. I was living in the void she had left behind. The worst part of it was going home. Being alone in the house. For the first time in my life.

I should have changed the music. Gotten rid of these grim thoughts with something Cuban. Guillermo Portabales. Francisco Repilado. Or better still, the Buena Vista Social Club. I should have. My life was full of should haves. Great, I thought, tooting my horn at the driver in front of me. He was calmly getting his family out of the car, along with everything they needed for a picnic on the beach. The icebox, the chairs, the folding table. All they needed was a TV set, I thought. My mood wasn't improving.

Coming level with the Café du Port, at the Pointe-Rouge—it had taken forty minutes to get that far—I felt like a drink. One or two. Maybe even three. But then I thought of

Fonfon and Honorine waiting for me on the terrace. I wasn't really alone. They were both there. With their love for me. Their patience. This morning, after the call from Hélène Pessayre, I'd left without saying hello.

"Who is it you want to kill?" Honorine had asked me last night.

"Forget it, Honorine. There are thousands of people I'd like to kill."

"Sure, but there seems to be one you've really set your heart on."

"Honestly, forget it. It's the heat. I'm on edge. Go back to sleep."

"Make yourself a camomile tea. It'll relax you. Fonfon had one."

I'd lowered my head. I didn't want to see the questions in her eyes. Or how afraid she was that I was getting involved in something I shouldn't. I still had a vivid memory of the way she'd looked at me four years ago when I'd told her that Ugo was dead. I didn't want to see that look again. Not for anything in the world. Especially not now.

Honorine knew I didn't have blood on my hands. She knew I'd never been able to bring myself to kill a man in cold blood. I'd let the cops handle Batisti. Narni had crashed his car at the bottom of a ravine on the Gineste pass. There was only Saadna. I'd let him burn, and hadn't felt any remorse. But I couldn't have killed even that loathsome piece of shit, just like that. She knew that. I'd told her all about it.

I wasn't the same man now. And Honorine knew that, too. There was too much repressed rage in me, too many scores I hadn't settled. And too much despair. I wasn't bitter, but I was weary. Tired. Tired of people, tired of the world. I couldn't get Sonia's unjust, stupid, cruel death out of my head. Her death made all other deaths unbearable. Including all the anonymous ones I read about every day in the newspapers.

Thousands. Hundreds of thousands. Ever since Bosnia. Rwanda. Now Algeria and its daily massacres. A hundred men, women and children slaughtered every night, their throats cut. Disgust.

Enough to make you throw up.

Sonia.

I didn't know what her killer looked like. I imagined a skull. Like on the skull and crossbones, which I saw being hoisted some nights in my head. Floating free, still unpunished. I wanted to have done with it. At least once. Once and for all.

Sonia.

Shit! I'd promised myself I'd go see her father and her son. That was what I should be doing this evening, not drinking. Seeing him and little Enzo. And telling them I thought I would have loved Sonia.

I put on the left indicator light, pulled out, and edged my car into the opposite lane. Immediately, people started hooting their horns. But I didn't give a damn. Nobody really gave a damn. They hooted for the hell of it. They screamed too, also for the hell of it.

"Where are you going, shithead?"

"To see your sister!"

After reversing twice, I managed to join the line, but I immediately turned left because I didn't want to get into any more jams. I zigzagged through a maze of side streets until I came out onto Avenue des Goumiers. The traffic was lighter here. I was on my way to La Capelette, a neighborhood that had been a magnet for Italian families, mainly from the North, ever since the twenties.

Sonia's father, Attilio, lived on Rue Antoine Del Bello, on the corner of Rue Fifi Turin. Two streets named for Italian resistance fighters who'd died for France. For freedom. For an idea of mankind that had nothing to do with the strutting of a Hitler or a Mussolini. Del Bello, who'd grown up in State custody in Italy, wasn't even French when he died in the maquis.

Attilio De Luca opened the door. I recognized him. Hassan was right. De Luca and I had met in his bar and had a few aperitifs together. He'd lost his job in 1992, after fifteen years as a timekeeper at Intramar. He'd been working on the waterfront for thirty-five years. He had told me a little about his life. How proud he'd been to be a longshoreman. The strikes he'd taken part in. Until the year the oldest of the long-shoremen were shown the door. The employers were modernizing the workforce. Not only the oldest had to go, but the troublemakers too. De Luca was on the red list. The workers who were considered "inflexible." And because of his age, he was among the first to be thrown out on the streets.

De Luca had been born on Rue Antoine Del Bello. A street where everyone's name ended in *i* or *a* before people called Alvarez, Gutierrez or Domenech started arriving.

"When I was born, out of a thousand people on that street, there were nine hundred and ninety-four Italians, two Spaniards and an Armenian."

His childhood memories were strangely similar to mine, and made me feel happy thinking about them.

"In summer, there'd be chairs set out all along the side-walk. Everyone had their little story to tell."

Dammit, I thought, why didn't he ever tell me about his daughter? Why didn't he ever bring her to Hassan's? Why did I see Sonia only once and then lose her forever? The terrible thing was that with Sonia, there were no regrets—the way there were with Lole—there was only remorse. The worst kind of remorse. Thinking I'd unwittingly brought about her death.

"Oh," De Luca said. "Montale."

He'd aged a hundred years.

"I heard about Sonia."

He looked up at me, and I saw how red his eyes were. They were also full of questions. Obviously, he didn't understand what I was doing here. You might feel close to someone over a *pastis* at Hassan's, but that didn't make you part of the family.

At the mention of Sonia's name, Enzo appeared. He only came up to his grandfather's waist. He clung to him and looked up at me. He had his mother's gray-blue eyes.

"I . . ."

"Come in, come in . . . Enzo, go back to bed! It's nearly ten o'clock . . . Kids never want to sleep," he said to me in a flat voice.

The room was quite large, but cluttered with furniture. Every surface was covered in trinkets, and family photos in frames. Just as his wife had left it, ten years ago, when she'd walked out on De Luca. Just as he hoped she'd find it when she returned. "She'll be back one day," he'd told me, full of hope.

"Sit down. Would you like a drink?"

"I'll have a *pastis*. In a large glass. I'm thirsty."

"Fucking heat," he said.

There wasn't much of an age difference between us. Maybe seven or eight years. I could almost have had a child Sonia's age. A girl. A boy. The thought of it made me uncomfortable.

He came back with two glasses, some ice cubes, and a big jug of water. Then he got the bottle out of a sideboard.

"Was it you she was supposed to be meeting last night?" he asked as he poured my drink.

"Yes."

"When I saw you at the door, I understood."

Seven or eight years' difference. The same generation, or almost. The generation that grew up after the war. That made sacrifices, that scrimped and saved. Pasta for lunch and dinner. And bread. Open bread, with tomato and olive oil. Bread and broccoli. Bread and eggplant. The generation that had plenty of dreams—dreams that, for our fathers, had worn the genial smile of Joseph Stalin. De Luca had joined the Communist Youth Movement at the age of fifteen.

"I swallowed it all," he'd told me. "Hungary, Czechoslovakia, the positive achievements of socialism."

He handed me the glass, without looking at me. I could guess what was going through his head. What he was feeling. His daughter in my arms. His daughter beneath me, as we made love. I didn't know if he'd really have liked it, the two of us together.

"Nothing happened, you know. We were supposed to meet, and . . ."

"Forget it, Montale. All that, now . . ."

He took a swig of his *pastis*, and finally looked at me. "Do you have children?"

"No."

"Then you can't understand."

I swallowed. His grief was clearly etched on his face, and hovered around his eyes. I was sure we'd have been friends, even if I'd started something with Sonia. I'd have invited him over for dinner with Fonfon and Honorine.

"I think she and I could have had something solid. With the boy."

"Have you ever been married?"

"No, never."

"You must have known a few women in your time."

"It's not what you think, De Luca."

"I don't think anything. In any case . . ." He emptied his glass. "Another one?"

"A small one."

"She was never happy. The only men she met were jerks. Can you explain it to me, Montale? Beautiful, intelligent, and never met anything but jerks. I won't even tell you about the last one, the father of . . ." He made a gesture with his head toward the room where Enzo was sleeping. "A good thing he walked out, or I'd have killed him sooner or later."

"There's no explanation."

"No. I think we spend our lives losing our way and by the time we find it, it's too late."

He looked at me again. There were the beginnings of tears in his eyes, but there was also a glimmer of friendship.

"My life exactly," I said.

My heart started pounding, then contracted. Somewhere, Lole must be squeezing it. She'd been a hundred per cent right about me, I didn't understand a thing. Loving another person surely meant showing yourself naked to that person. Naked in your strength, and in your weakness. Was that what scared me about love? The nakedness of it? The truth of it? Truth itself?

I'd have told Sonia everything. Even that contraction in my heart whose name was Lole. Yes, as I'd just told De Luca, Sonia and I could have had something solid. Something different. Joy and laughter. Happiness. But different. It had to be different. When the woman you've dreamed about, waited for, desired for years, then met and loved, leaves you, you can't imagine you'll meet her again like that, on some other street corner of your life. Everyone knows there's no lost property office for love.

Sonia would have understood. She hadn't taken long to make my heart speak, or just to make me speak. And perhaps there would have been a future for us. A future true to our desires.

"Yes," De Luca said, again emptying his glass.

I stood up.

"Is that all you came here for—to tell me it was you?"

"Yes," I lied. "To tell you that."

Painfully, he got to his feet.

"Does the boy know?"

"Not yet. I don't know how . . . And I don't know how I'm going to manage with him . . . I mean, one night, one day. One week, during the vacation . . . But bringing him up? I wrote to my wife . . ."

"Can I go say good night to him?"

De Luca nodded. But then he put his hand on my arm. All the sadness in him was about to explode. His chest rose. He'd put up a barrier of pride around him, and now the tears were bursting through.

"Why?" He started crying. "Why did they kill her? Why her?"

"I don't know," I said, in a very low voice.

I drew him to me, and held him in my arms. He was sobbing loudly. I said again as low as possible, "I don't know."

His tears of love for Sonia—big, hot, sticky tears—ran down my neck. They stank of death. The same stench I'd smelled the other night, going into Hassan's. Exactly the same smell. In my mind's eye, I tried to put a face to Sonia's killer.

Then I saw Enzo, standing there in front of us, holding a little teddy bear under his arm.

"Why's Grandpa crying?"

I freed myself from De Luca, squatted in front of Enzo, and put my arms around his shoulders.

"Your mommy won't be coming back," I said. "She . . . she had an accident. Do you understand, Enzo? She's dead."

And I started crying too. Crying for us, who would have to survive all this. The world's ever-present corruption.

10.

IN WHICH BEING LIGHT CAN RECONCILE SADNESS WITH THE FLIGHT OF A SEAGULL

Fonfon, Honorine and I had played rummy until midnight. Playing cards with those two was more than a pleasure. It was a way to get closer. To share feelings we found hard to express in words. As we played, we exchanged looks, smiles. And although it was a simple game, you had to keep track of the cards the others had played. It was a good opportunity to keep my mind off things for a few hours.

Fonfon had brought along a bottle of Bunan. An old stemmed *marc* from La Cadière, near Bandol.

"Taste this," he'd said. "It'll make a change from that Scotch of yours."

It was delicious. Quite different from my Lagavulin with its slightly peaty taste. The Bunan was dry, but extremely fruity, smelling of scrubland. By the time I'd won two games of rummy and lost eight, I'd already enjoyed four little glasses of it.

As we were saying good night, Honorine came up to me with a padded envelope.

"I almost forgot. The postman left this for you this morning. As it was marked fragile, he didn't want to put it in your mail box."

There was no indication of the sender on the back. The postmark said Saint-Jean-du-Gard. I opened the envelope and took out five computer disks. Two blue, one white, one red, one black. *I still love you*, Babette had written on a sheet of paper. And underneath: *Take good care of this for me.*

Babette! The blood started beating in my temples. At the same time, Sonia's face flashed in front of me. Sonia with her throat cut. I had a clear memory of Sonia's neck. Tanned, like her skin. Thin. It looked as soft as the shoulder where I'd placed my hand for a brief moment. A neck it would have been nice to kiss, there, just below the ear. Or stroke with your fingertips, and marvel at the softness. How I'd have liked to hate Babette!

But how do you go about hating someone you love? Or someone you once loved? A friend or a lover. Mavros or Lole. I couldn't do it, any more than I could have done without the friendship of Manu and Ugo. You can stop yourself seeing them, keeping in touch with them, but you can't hate them, it's impossible. For me at least.

I reread Babette's note, and felt the weight of the disks. This was it, I thought, our fates were linked, in the most horrible way possible. Babette was appealing to love, but it was death that was rearing its head. To the death. That's what we used to say when we were kids. We'd make a little cut in our wrists, and cross our forearms, so that one's person's wrist was against the other's, and our blood mingled. Friends for life. Brothers. We'd always love each other.

Babette. For years, we'd brought each other nothing but our mutual desire. And our mutual solitude. Her words *I still love you* made me uncomfortable. They didn't strike a chord with me. Was she sincere? I wondered. Or was it the only way she knew to call for help? I was only too well aware that you could say things, think they were true in the moment you said them, and then do things, in the hours or days that followed, that belied them. Especially in love. Because love is the most irrational of feelings, and its source—whatever people say—is in the meeting of two bodies, and the pleasure they give each other.

One day, Lole had packed her bag, and said, "I'm going away. I may be gone for a week."

I looked at her for a long time, my stomach in knots. Usually, she would say things like, "I'm going to see my mother," or "My sister isn't well. I'm going to Toulouse for a few days."

"I need to think, Fabio. I really need it. For myself. You understand, I need to think about myself."

She was tense, having to say it like that. She'd have liked to find a better moment to tell me, to explain. I understood her tension, even though it hurt me. I'd been planning—but as usual, I hadn't said anything—to take her on an excursion into the countryside inland from Nice. Over toward Gorbio, Sainte-Agnes, Sospel.

"If that's what you want to do."

She was leaving to join her friend. The guitarist she'd met at a concert in Seville, when she was visiting with her mother. She hadn't told me until she got back.

"I didn't do anything to . . ." she'd said. "I didn't think it would happen so fast, Fabio."

I held her in my arms. Her body felt stiff against mine. I knew then that she'd been thinking a lot about us, and about herself. But of course not the way I'd imagined. Nor the way I'd heard in what she'd said before she left.

"What are those?" Honorine asked.

"Computer disks."

"Do you know about that kind of thing?"

"A little. I used to have a computer in my office."

I embraced the two of them and said good night. I was in a hurry to go.

"Even if you leave early," Fonfon said, "come and see me first."

"I promise."

I was already thinking about something else. About the disks and what was in them. The reason for the mess Babette was in. The mess she was dragging me into. Whatever it was had cost Sonia her life. And had delivered a knockout blow to an eight-year-old boy and his poor lost grandfather.

*

I called Hassan. When he picked up, I recognized the first notes of "In a Sentimental Mood" in the background. I recognized the sound, too. John Coltrane and Duke Ellington. A real gem.

"Is Sébastien there, by any chance?"

"Sure. I'll call him over."

Over the years, I'd gotten friendly with a group of friends who often came to Hassan's. Sébastien, Mathieu, Régis and Cédric. They were all twenty-five. Mathieu and Régis were finishing their architecture studies. Cédric was a painter, and had recently been organizing techno concerts. Sébastien was moonlighting on construction sites. The friendship between them warmed my heart. You could almost touch it, even if you couldn't explain it. That was how I'd been with Manu and Ugo. We'd stagger every night from one bar to the next, laughing about everything, even the girls we were going out with. We were different and yet we had the same dreams. Just like these four young guys. And like them, we knew that we couldn't have had the same conversations with anyone else.

"Yes?" Sébastien said.

"Montale here. I'm not breaking anything up, I hope?"

"No. The girls are washing their hair. There's just the four of us here."

"Your cousin Cyril. Do you think he could open some disks for me?"

Sébastien had told me Cyril was a computer freak. With an incredible amount of equipment. Always surfing the net at night.

"No sweat. When?"

"Now."

"Now? Shit, man, this is worse than when you were a cop!"

"You said it."

"O.K. We'll wait for you. We still have four rounds on account!"

It took me less than twenty minutes to get there. All the lights were green, except for three that I ran when they were still amber. There were no traffic cops around. Hassan's bar wasn't exactly packed. Sébastien and his friends. Three couples. And a regular, a tired looking man of about thirty who came in every week to read *Taktik*, the free cultural paper, from cover to cover. I assumed he couldn't actually afford a ticket to a concert, or even a movie.

"If you can get rid of them for me," Hassan said, indicating the four young guys, "I'll be able to close."

"Cyril's expecting us," Sébastien said. "Whenever you like. He lives just around the corner. Boulevard Chave."

"Can I buy you all another round?"

"Well, if we're working at night, that's the least we can expect."

"Right, this is the last one," Hassan said. "Bring your glasses."

He poured me a whisky. Without asking. The same kind he'd served Sonia. An Oban. He made an exception and poured himself one too. He raised his glass as if in a toast. We looked at each other. We were thinking the same thing. About the same person. We didn't need words. It was the same way with Fonfon and Honorine. There are no words to speak about Evil.

Hassan had let the Coltrane-Ellington album run on. The track called *Angelica* was just starting. A track all about love. Joy. Happiness. So light, it could reconcile any human sadness with the flight of a seagull to other shores.

"Another one?"

"A quick one. A round for the boys, too."

The five disks contained pages and pages of documents. They had been compressed to contain as much information as possible.

"Will you be O.K.?" Cyril asked.

I was sitting in front of his computer, starting to scroll through the files on the blue disks. "I'll only need an hour. I'm not going to read everything. Just find a few things I need."

"Take your time. We have enough here to withstand a siege!"

They'd brought back several six-packs of beer, pizzas, and enough cigarettes to last all night. The way they'd started, they were going to remake the world four or five times over. And, given what I was seeing in front of my eyes right now, the world could certainly do with being remade.

Out of curiosity, I opened the first file. *How organized crime is poisoning the world economy.* This was clearly a draft of Babette's report.

In an era of globalized markets, the role of organized crime in the market economy is still little known. Public opinion, nourished by Hollywood stereotypes and sensational journalism, associates criminal activity with the collapse of public order. The activities of petty criminals are constantly talked about, but the political and economic role, as well as the influence of international criminal organizations, is rarely brought out into the open.

I scrolled down.

Organized crime is inextricably interwoven with the economic system. The opening up of world markets, the decline of the Welfare State, privatization, the deregulation of international finance and trade: all these things have tended to favor the growth of illegal activities as well as the internationalization of a rival criminal economy.

According to the United Nations, the annual world income of trans-national criminal organizations is in the region of a thousand billion dollars, a figure equivalent to the combined gross national product of those countries categorized by the World

Bank as low-income and their three billion inhabitants. This estimate takes into account both the revenue from drug trafficking, illegal arms sales, smuggling of nuclear materials, etc., and the revenue from activities controlled by the Mafia, such as prostitution, gambling, and the black market in currency.

What it does not take into account, however, is the extent to which criminal organizations have taken control of legitimate businesses, or the extent to which they dominate the means of production in many sectors of the legal economy.

I was starting to get an idea of what the other disks might contain. There were footnotes referring to official documents. Another set of notes, in bold lettering, contained cross-references to the other disks, classified by transaction, by place, by company, by political party, and finally by name. Fargette. Yann Piat. Noriega. Sun Investment. International Bankers, Luxembourg . . . It made my flesh creep. Because I was sure Babette had worked with that professional dedication that had driven her ever since she had started out as a journalist. That fierce determination to get at the truth.

I scrolled again.

Criminal organizations work unofficially with legal businesses, investing in a variety of legitimate activities that provide them not only with a cover for money laundering but also with the means to accumulate capital outside their criminal activities. These investments are mainly in the fields of luxury real estate, the leisure industries, publishing and media, financial services, etc., as well as in industry, agriculture and public services.

"I'm making spaghetti bolognese," Sébastien interrupted me. "Would you like some?"

"Only if you change the music!"

"Did you hear that, Cédric?" Sébastien called.

"We'll see what we can do!" Cédric replied.

The music stopped.

"Listen to this, it's Ben Harper."

I didn't know it, but what the hell? It was bearable.

Before I stood up, I read one last sentence: *The results achieved by organized crime surpass those of most of the companies in Fortune magazine's Top 500, and their organizations are more like General Motors than the traditional Sicilian Mafia.* It was a whole master plan that Babette had decided to take on.

"So where have you gotten to?" I asked, sitting down at the table.

"Nowhere in particular," Cédric replied.

"Whichever way you look at things," Mathieu argued, "we always come back to the same place. Where we are now. In the shit."

"Well spotted," I said. "What do you do about it?"

Sébastien laughed. "Well, when you walk, the important thing is not to get it everywhere."

Everyone laughed. So did I. But my laughter was a little forced. Because that was exactly where I was, in the shit, and I wasn't really sure I wasn't getting it everywhere.

"Great spaghetti," I said.

"Sébastien takes after his father," Cyril said. "He loves cooking for other people."

The reason for Babette's problems must be on one of the other disks. The one where she listed the names of politicians and heads of companies. The black disk.

The white was a compilation of documents. The red contained interviews and testimonies. Including an interview with Bernard Bertossa, the chief prosecutor of Geneva.

"In your opinion, is France doing enough to combat international corruption, at least at the European level?"

"Of all the European countries, only Italy has developed a genuine policy to combat dirty money and corruption. Particularly at the time of the Mani pulite operation. To be hon-

est, France doesn't give the impression she really wants to tackle money laundering or influence peddling. There's no real political strategy to deal with these things, there are only individual judges or prosecutors who put a lot of effort into their cases and obstinately see them through. Things are starting to change in Spain, where a special prosecutor's department has just been created to fight corruption. But nothing like that exists in France. And it has nothing to do with which party we're talking about, or whether or not they're in power. They all have skeletons in their cupboards, but they don't want to admit it."

I didn't have the strength to look at the black disk. What would be the point? My vision of the world was black enough as it was.

"Can I have a set of copies?" I asked Cyril.

"As many as you like."

Then, remembering the things Sébastien had told me about the Internet, I added, "And is it possible to put all of it on the Internet?"

"Create a Web site, you mean?"

"Yes, something that anyone could look at."

"Sure."

"Could you do that? Create a Web site for me, and only get it going if I ask you."

"I'll do it tomorrow."

I left them at three in the morning, after a last beer. Once out on the boulevard, I lit a cigarette, and crossed Place Jean-Jaurès, which was completely deserted. For the first time in a long time, I didn't feel safe.

11.

IN WHICH IT'S LIFE THAT'S AT STAKE, TO THE LAST BREATH

I woke with a start. A little bell had rung in my head. But it wasn't the phone. It wasn't a noise in the house either. It really had been in my head, and it wasn't really a bell. More like a click. Had I been dreaming? What about? It was only five to six. Shit! I stretched. I already knew I wouldn't get back to sleep now.

I got up, and went out on the terrace, an unlit cigarette in my hand. The sea was dark blue, almost black, and restless. The mistral was starting. A bad sign. In summer, the mistral meant one thing—forest fires. Hundreds of acres of forest and scrub went up in smoke every year. The firefighters must already be gearing up for trouble.

Saint-Jean-du-Gard, I told myself. That was it. The click. The postmark on Babette's envelope had said Saint-Jean-du-Gard. In the Cévennes. What the hell was she doing there? Who was she staying with? I'd made coffee, in my little one-cup Italian coffee maker. One cup after another. That was how I liked it. I didn't like reheated coffee. I finally lit my cigarette, and took a gentle drag on it. It went down well. A good omen for the ones to follow.

I put on a CD by the South African pianist Abdullah Ibrahim. *Echoes from Africa*. One piece in particular. "*Zikr.*" I didn't have any religious beliefs. But there was such serenity in the vocals on that track—a duet with his bassist, Johnny Dyani—it made you want to praise the earth and its beauty. I'd spent hours listening to that piece. At dawn or at sunset. It made me feel human.

The music swelled. I stood framed by the French window,

with my cup in my hand, and looked at the sea, which was more agitated now. I didn't understand any of the words Abdullah Ibrahim was singing, but I translated that "Remembrance of Allah" in my own way. It's my life that's at stake here, on this earth. A life with the taste of hot stones, the sighing of the sea, the song of the cicadas. To my last breath, I will love this life. *Insh'Allah*.

A seagull flew past, very low, almost at the level of the terrace. I thought of Hélène Pessayre. A pretty seagull. I didn't have the right to lie to her anymore. Now that I was in possession of Babette's disks. Now that I had an idea where she was holed up. I had to check, but I was almost certain. Saint-Jean-du-Gard. In the Cévennes. I opened her binder of articles.

It was her first big story. The only one I hadn't yet read. I suppose because of the accompanying photos, which Babette had taken herself. Photos full of affection for the former philosophy student who'd left Paris after May '68 to raise goats. She'd loved this guy Bruno, I was sure of it. Like me. Maybe she'd loved him and me at the same time. And others too.

So what? I asked myself, as I read the article. That was ten years ago. But did she still love you? Did she really still love you? That note of hers bugged me. *I still love you.* Was it possible to start your life over again with someone you once loved? Someone you'd lived with? No, I didn't believe that. I'd never believed it about the women I'd left or who'd left me. I didn't believe it about Babette either. The only woman I could imagine getting back together with was Lole, and that was pure insanity. A woman I'd known—I couldn't remember her name—had told me once that you mustn't disturb the ghosts of love.

Le Castellas. That was it. That's where she was. I was sure of it. The way Babette described it, it was the ideal place to hide out. Except that you couldn't lie low for the rest of your life. Unless you decided, like this Bruno, to start a new life there. But I couldn't see Babette raising goats. She still had too much anger in her.

I made myself a third cup of coffee, then called Information, and got the number of Le Castellas. At the fifth ring, someone lifted the receiver. A child's voice. A boy.

"Who is that?"

"I'd like to speak to your daddy."

"Mommy!" he cried.

Footsteps.

"Hello?"

"Hello. I'd like to speak to Bruno."

"Who shall I say is calling?"

"Montale. Fabio Montale. He doesn't know me."

"Just a moment."

More footsteps. A door opening. Then Bruno's voice came on the line.

"Yes. What is it?"

I liked his voice. Determined, confident. As rugged as the mountains.

"You don't know me. I'm a friend of Babette's. I'd like to speak to her."

Silence. He was thinking.

"Who did you say?"

"Listen, let's stop this play acting. I know she's hiding at your place. Tell her Montale called. Ask her to call me back as soon as possible."

"What's going on?"

"Tell her to call me. Thanks."

Babette called half an hour later.

Outside, the mistral was blowing hard. I'd gone out to fold my sunshade, and Honorine's. She hadn't yet appeared. She must have gone to Fonfon's to have a coffee and read *La Marseillaise*. Ever since *Le Provençal* and *Le Méridional* had merged into a single newspaper called *La Provence*, Fonfon had been buying only *La Marseillaise*. He didn't like newspapers that sat on the fence. He liked ones that took a stand. Even if he didn't share their ideas. Like *La Marseillaise*, which was a Communist paper. Or like *Le Méridional*, which before moving to the centre-right had made its fortune, about twenty years ago, spreading the extreme racist ideas of the National Front.

Fonfon couldn't understand how the editorial in *La Provence* could be left-wing one day and right-wing the next, depending on which of the editors had written it.

"That's pluralism for you!" he'd shouted.

Then he'd shown me that day's editorial: a tribute to the Pope, who was visiting France. The editorial praised the moral virtues of Christianity.

"I mean, I got nothing against the Pope. Or against the guy who wrote this. People can write what they like, it's a free country. But . . ." He turned the pages. "Here, read this."

There was a small item in the local pages, with photographs, about a guy who'd opened a new restaurant on the coast. This guy was talking about how great his place was, because all the waitresses were young and pretty and walked around almost naked. He didn't say that you could put your hand on their asses, but he implied it. It was the ideal place for a business meal. Money and sex have always made good bedfellows.

"No, you can't be blessed by the Pope on page one, and get a blowjob on page four!"

"Fonfon!"

"Hell, a newspaper without morality isn't a newspaper. I'm not buying it anymore, and that's that. It's over."

Since then, the only paper he'd read was *La Marseillaise*. And that also made him angry sometimes. Sometimes a little insincerely. But often with good reason. You couldn't change the way he was. But I liked him like that. I'd met too many people who were all talk and no substance.

I'd jumped when the phone rang. For I moment I thought it might not be Babette, but the Mafia guys.

"Fabio," she said.

There was a tremendous amount of fear and weariness in her voice. Just from the way she spoke my name, I realized she'd changed. It suddenly came home to me that, before going on the run, she must have been through a really hard time.

"Yes."

A silence. I didn't know what she was thinking about during that silence. I was thinking about all the nights we'd made love. If you look back, that woman whose name I couldn't remember had also said, you end up falling to the bottom of a well. I was at the edge of the well. On the rim. Babette.

"Fabio," she said again, more confidently.

Sonia's corpse again came into my head. In all its weight and coldness. Emptying my mind of all other thoughts, all other memories.

"Babette, we have to talk."

"Did you get the disks?"

"I've read them. Most of them, anyway. Last night."

"What do you think? I did a good job, didn't I?"

"Babette. Stop with that. The guys who are after you are on my back."

"Oh!" Fear gripped her throat, strangling her words. "I don't know what to do anymore, Fabio."

"Come back."

"Come back?" She sounded almost hysterical. "Are you crazy? They murdered Gianni. In Rome. And his brother Francesco. And his friend Beppe. And—"

"They killed a woman I loved, right here," I said, raising my voice. "And they'll kill others, other people I love. And then they'll kill me. And sooner or later they'll kill you. You can't stay in hiding up there forever."

Another silence. I loved Babette's face. Quite a round face, framed by long, chestnut-red hair, curly at the ends. A Botticelli face.

I cleared my throat. "We can come to some kind of arrangement."

"What?" she cried. "Fabio, that report is my life's work! If you've looked at the disks, you must have realized the amount of work I did. So just what kind of arrangement do you think we can come to, huh?"

"An arrangement with life. Or death. Your choice."

"Stop it! I'm not in the mood for philosophizing."

"Neither am I. I just want to stay alive. And keep you alive."

"Oh, sure. If I come there, I'm signing my death warrant."

"Maybe not."

"Is that right? So what do you suggest?"

I felt my anger rising. The wind was blowing harder than ever outside. "Fuck it, Babette! You're dragging everyone into this fucking investigation of yours. Doesn't that bother you? Can you sleep at night? Can you eat? Can you fuck? Huh? Answer me, damn you! Do you like it that my friends are getting whacked? And that I might be whacked, too? Huh? Fuck it! And you tell me you still love me! You're crazy, you know, you're a fucking crazy woman!"

She burst into tears. "You have no right to talk to me like that!"

"Yes, I do! I loved that woman, dammit! Her name was Sonia, she was thirty-four years old, and I hadn't met anyone like her for years. So I have every right!"

"Go to hell!"

She hung up.

Georges Mavros had been murdered that morning, about seven. I didn't find out until two hours later. My line was still busy. When the phone rang, I thought it was Babette calling back.

"Montale."

The tone was harsh. A police captain's tone. Hélène Pessayre. Trouble again, I thought. And by trouble, I meant that she'd start bugging me again to tell her what I was hiding. But she had something to tell me, and she wasn't wearing kid gloves.

"Your friend Georges Mavros was killed this morning when he got home. He was found in the ring, with his throat cut. Just like Sonia. Do you still have nothing to tell me?"

Georges. Like an idiot, my first thought was of Pascale. But he hadn't heard from Pascale in six months. He had no children. Mavros was alone. Like me. I sincerely hoped he'd had a happy night, a beautiful night, with his friend from Réunion.

"I'm coming over there."

"Come right now!" Hélène Pessayre ordered. "To the gym. That way, you can identify him. I think you owe him that at least."

"I'm on my way," I replied, my voice breaking.

I hung up. The phone rang.

"Did you hear about your pal?"

The killer.

"I just heard."

"A pity." He laughed. "I'd have liked to be the one to tell you. But the cops don't waste any time these days."

I didn't say anything. I was immersing myself in his voice, as if it might help me to make an identikit picture of him.

"Attractive woman, that cop, isn't she? Montale, are you listening?"

"Yeah."

"Don't try any tricks. With her or anyone else. Cop or otherwise. Or we'll just get through the list a little quicker. You understand what I'm saying?"

"I understand. No tricks."

"But you were having a stroll with her yesterday, right? What were you planning to do, fuck her?"

They were there, I told myself. They were following me. That's it, they're following me. That's how they got on to Sonia. And Mavros. They don't have any list. They don't know anything about me. They're following me and, depending on their estimate of how close I am to someone, they kill that person. That's all. Except that Fonfon and Honorine had to be at the top of the list. These guys must have registered how fond I was of those two.

"Montale, how far have you gotten with the shit stirrer?"

"I have a lead," I said. "I'll know by this evening."

"Congratulations. Talk to you this evening, then."

For a few moments, I took my head in my hands, to think. But there was nothing to think about. I redialed Bruno's number. He picked up the phone himself this time. They must have been having a council of war in Le Castellas.

"This is Montale again."

A silence, then, "She doesn't want to speak to you."

"Tell her if I come up there, I'll kill her. Tell her that."

"I heard," Babette growled. They'd put on the speaker.

"They killed Mavros this morning!" I cried. "You remember Mavros, don't you, for Christ's sake? The nights we spent with him? The fun we had?"

"What should I do?" she asked.

"What do you mean, what should you do?"

"When I get to Marseilles. What should I do?"

How was I supposed to know what she should do? I hadn't even given it a moment's thought. I didn't have a plan. I just wanted it to end. I wanted the people close to me to be left alone. I closed my eyes. I didn't want Fonfon and Honorine to be touched. That was all that mattered.

Apart from killing that son of a bitch.

"I'll call you later and tell you. Ciao."

"Fabio . . ."

I hung up, cutting her off.

I put on *Zikr* again. I needed that music to soothe the chaos inside me. To assuage the hate that couldn't be assuaged. I fingered the ring Didier Perez had given me, and once again translated Abdullah Ibrahim's prayer in my own fashion. Yes, I love this life to distraction and I want to live it as a free man. *Insh'Allah*, Montale.

12.

IN WHICH THE QUESTION ARISES OF HOW TO LIVE IN A SOCIETY WITHOUT MORALITY

I looked around the gym. Everything in it was familiar to me. The ring, the smell, the dim lighting. The punching bags, the dumbbells. The yellow walls hung with posters. Everything was just the way we'd left it the night before. The towels on the bench, the bandages hanging from the horizontal bar.

I could hear the voice of Mavros's father, Takis.

"Come on, boy, come and get me!"

How old was I? Maybe twelve. Mavros had said, "My father will train you." My head was full of images of Marcel Cerdan. My idol. My father's too. I dreamed about being a boxer. But learning to box meant, first and foremost, learning to overcome my physical fear, learning to take the blows, learning to give them. To be respected. That was something you really needed on the street. And it was how my friendship with Manu had started—with fisticuffs. Rue du Refuge, in the Panier. One evening when I was walking home with my beautiful cousin Gélou. He'd called me a wop, the lousy spic! It was just an excuse to start a fight and attract Gélou's attention.

"Go on, hit me!" Takis was saying.

I'd punched him, timidly.

"Harder, dammit! Harder! Go on, I'm used to it."

He was offering me his cheek to hit. I'd punched him again. Then again. And then another one. A direct, well-placed blow. Takis Mavros had appreciated that.

"Go on, son."

I'd punched him again, really hard this time, and he'd dodged the blow. My nose hit his hard, muscular shoulder.

The blood started to gush out, and I watched, dazed, as the drops fell on the ring.

The ring was covered in blood.

I couldn't take my eyes off it. Fuck, Georges, I thought, we didn't even have a chance to get plastered one last time!

"Montale."

It was Hélène Pessayre. She'd placed a hand on my shoulder. The heat of her palm went right through my body. It felt good. I turned to face her. There was a hint of sadness in her black eyes, and a lot of anger.

"We need to talk."

She looked around her. The gym was full of people. I'd already spotted the two cops in her team. Alain Béraud had waved at me. A gesture that was meant to be friendly.

"In there," I said, pointing to the little room Mavros had used as an office.

She strode toward it. This morning, her jeans were sea-green and her T-shirt was wide and black and covered her ass. I guessed she was packing a gun today.

She opened the door, ushered me in, and closed the door behind her. For a fraction of a second, we stared at each other. We were almost the same height. Her slap hit me full in the face, before I'd even had time to take out a cigarette. The violence of the blow, and my surprise, made me drop the pack. I bent down to pick it up. It was by her feet. My cheek was burning. I stood up and looked at her. She didn't flinch.

"I really wanted to do that," she said coolly. Then, in the same tone, "Sit down."

I remained standing. "That's the first time I've ever been slapped. By a woman, I mean."

"If you want it to be the last time, you need to tell me everything, Montale. I respect you, because of what I've heard about you. But I'm not Loubet. I don't have any time to waste having you followed, or speculating about how much you know. I want the truth. I told you yesterday, I hate lies."

"You also told me you wouldn't forgive me if I lied to you."

"I'm giving you a second chance."

A second death, a second chance. The last one. Like a last life. We looked hard at each other. It wasn't open war between us yet.

"Here," I said. And I put Babette's five disks on the table. The first set of copies Cyril had made for me during the night. He'd really gotten the bit between his teeth. While he worked, Sébastien and his friends had played me tracks by the latest Marseilles rap bands. My knowledge didn't go beyond IAM and Massilia Sound System. Apparently, I was behind the times.

They introduced me to the Fonky Family, young guys from the Panier and Belzunce—who'd been part of the Bad Boys of Marseilles—and Third Eye, who were straight out of North Marseilles. Rap wasn't really my thing, but I was always amazed by the content. How relevant what they said was. How cleverly they used words. What they sang about was the lives of their friends, on the street or in the joint. And how easy it was to die. And how many kids ended up in mental hospitals. It was a reality I'd been close to for years.

"What are these?" Hélène Pessayre asked, without touching the disks.

"The most up to date summary of the activities of the Mafia. Enough to start a fire all the way from Marseilles to Nice."

"As bad as that?" she replied, deliberately incredulous.

"So bad that if you read it, you won't want to spend too much time at police headquarters. You'll be wondering who's going to shoot you in the back."

"You mean there are cops involved?"

She was as calm as ever. I didn't know what kind of inner

strength she had, but it seemed as if nothing could shake her. Like Loubet. The opposite of me. Maybe that was why I'd never been a good cop. I was too sensitive.

"Lots of people are involved. Politicians, industrialists, businessmen. It's all here: their names, how much they've made, which banks their money's in, the account numbers, all that kind of thing. As for the cops . . ."

She'd sat down, and I did the same.

"Can I have a cigarette?"

I held out my pack. She took a cigarette and I lit it for her. She put her hand on mine to bring the lighter closer to her.

"What about the cops?"

"Let's just say they have a good working relationship with the Mafia. Especially when it comes to passing on information."

For years, according to Babette's file on the Var, Jean-Louis Fargette had paid police officers a good price to tap the phones of certain politicians. Just to make sure that they weren't cheating him out of the commission they were supposed to pay him. And to put pressure on them if it became necessary. Some of the phone taps provided details about their private lives. Their families. Their sexual preferences. Which ones used prostitutes. Which ones were pedophiles.

Hélène Pessayre took a long drag on her cigarette. Like Lauren Bacall, only more natural. Her face was turned to me, but her eyes were lost in the distance. In some place where, I supposed, she had her reasons for being a cop.

"What else?" she said, her eyes coming back to me.

"Everything you've always wanted to know . . ."

I remembered another section of Babette's draft report. *There has been a fundamental change in the structures of post-war capitalism, and legal and illegal businesses are increasingly interconnected. The Mafia invests in legitimate businesses and, at the same time, these businesses channel financial resources*

towards the criminal economy, by taking over banks or com-
mercial enterprises involved in money laundering or with
strong links to criminal organizations.

The banks claim that these transactions are carried out in
good faith and that their directors are unaware of the source of
the funds deposited. Not only do the big banks agree to launder
money, in return for substantial commissions, but they also
lend money to criminal organizations, rather than investing in
genuine industrial or agricultural concerns.

There is a close connection, Babette wrote, *between world*
debt, illegal trade and money laundering. Since the debt crisis at
the beginning of the 1980s, the price of raw materials has plum-
meted, bringing about a dramatic downturn in the fortunes of
developing countries. As a result of austerity measures imposed
by international creditors, state employees have been dismissed,
nationalized companies sold off, public investment frozen, and
funds to farmers and industrialists reduced. With rampant
unemployment and falling wages, the legal economy is in crisis.

This was the point we'd reached, I'd told myself during
the night, reading these words. What we called the future was
all mapped out. A new age of human misery. How much had
they fined that housewife who'd stolen a few steaks from a
supermarket? How many months of prison had they given
those kids in Strasbourg for breaking windows on buses and
in bus shelters?

I remembered what Fonfon had said. A newspaper without morality isn't a newspaper anymore. Right, and a society
without morality isn't a society anymore. Same with a country. It was easier to send the cops to throw the committees of
the unemployed out of welfare offices than to tackle the roots
of the evil. This corruption that was eating away at mankind.

"More than two years ago we froze money that came from a
big drug deal in France," Bernard Bertossa, the public prosecutor of Geneva, said at the end of his interview with Babette.

"The perpetrators have been sentenced, but the French legal system still hasn't presented any demand for restitution, despite repeated requests."

Yes, this was the point we'd reached, the lowest point of morality.

I looked at Hélène Pessayre. "It'd take too long to explain. Read it if you can. I didn't get any farther than the list of names. I didn't really have the guts to know the rest. I wasn't sure that, if I did, I'd still feel happy sitting on my terrace looking at the sea."

She smiled. "Where did you get these disks?"

"A friend of mine sent them to me. A journalist named Babette Bellini. She's spent the last few years investigating all this. It's an obsession."

"How are the deaths of Sonia De Luca and Georges Mavros connected with this?"

"The Mafia don't know where Babette is. They'd like to get their hands on her. There are certain papers they want to get back. I think it's the lists they're interested in. The lists of banks, individual account numbers."

I closed my eyes for a moment and saw Babette, her smile. "Then they'll kill her, of course," I said.

"And where do you fit in?"

"The killers have asked me to find her. As an incentive, they're killing off the people I love. And they're going to carry on until they get to the people who mean the most to me."

"Did you love Sonia?"

There was no harshness in her voice now. She was a woman talking to a man. About a man and another woman. Almost as if we were old friends.

I shrugged. "I wanted to see her again."

"Is that all?"

"No, that's not all," I replied sharply.

"What else?"

She was sympathetic but insistent. Forcing me to talk about what I'd felt that night. My stomach clenched.

"It wasn't just desire!" I said, raising my voice. "Do you understand? I really felt we might have a future. We might even live together."

"All in one night?"

"One night or a hundred, one look or a thousand, it makes no difference." By now, I wanted to scream.

"Montale," she said quietly, and her voice had a calming effect on me. I liked the way she said my name. It seemed to carry in it all the joy, all the laughter of her summers in Algiers.

"I think you know immediately, when you meet someone, if you just want to get laid, or to start something real. Don't you?"

"Yes, I think so, too," she said, without taking her eyes off me. "Are you unhappy, Montale?"

Fuck! Did I have unhappiness written all over my face? Sonia had said the same thing to Honorine the other day. Now Hélène Pessayre was flinging the word at me. Had Lole really drained me of happiness? Had she really taken all my dreams away with her? All my reasons for living? Or was it just that I didn't know where to find them inside me?

After Pascale left him, Mavros had told me, "You know, it was like she was turning the pages really fast. Five years of laughter, joy, shouting matches sometimes, love, tenderness, nights, mornings, siestas, dreams, journeys . . . Until we got to the words The End. Which she wrote herself, with her own hand. And then she took the book away with her. And I . . ."

He was crying. I listened to him in silence. Helpless, faced with so much pain.

"And now I've lost my reason for living. I'd never loved a woman the way I loved Pascale. She was the only one, Fabio, the only one, Goddammit! Now I'm just going through the motions. Because you have to do things. That's what life is. Doing things. But in my head, there's nothing left. Or in my heart." He'd put his finger on his head, then his heart. "Nothing."

I didn't know what to say. There was nothing you could say in response to something like that. As I was to find out when Lole left.

That night, I'd taken Mavros home with me. Stopping off along the way at a whole lot of bars in the harbor area. From the Café de la Mairie to the Bar de la Marine. Hassan's, too, for a while.

I'd laid him on the couch, with my bottle of Lagavulin within easy reach. "Will you be O.K.?"

"I have everything I need," he'd said, pointing to the bottle.

Then I'd left him and slipped into bed against Lole's warm, soft body. I lay with my cock against her buttocks and one hand on her breast, holding her the way a child learning to swim holds on to his rubber ring. Clinging on for dear life. It was only Lole's love that kept my head above water. Otherwise, I'd have sunk. Or been carried away by the current.

"You still haven't answered," Hélène Pessayre said.

"I think I need a lawyer."

She laughed, which did me good.

There was a knock at the door.

"Yes?"

It was Béraud, from her team.

"We've finished, captain." He looked at me. "Can he identify him?"

"Yes," I said. "I'll do it."

"Give us a few more minutes, Alain."

He went out and closed the door.

Hélène Pessayre stood up and took a few steps around the cramped office. Then she came and stood in front of me. "If you found this Babette Bellini, would you tell me?"

"Yes," I replied, without hesitation, looking her straight in the eyes.

I stood up too. We were face to face, the way we'd been before she slapped me. There was a vital question I had to ask her. "And what do we do then? If I find her?"

For the first time, I sensed an uncertainty in her. As if she knew what I was going to say next.

"You'd give her police protection. Is that it? Until you arrested the killers, if you could find them. And then what? What happens when other killers arrive? And then others?"

It was my way of slapping her in the face. Cops didn't like to hear they were powerless.

"You'll be transferred before that happens, not to Saint-Brieuc, like Loubet, but to Argenton-sur-Creuse or some other one-horse town!"

She went pale, and I regretted losing my temper with her. It was a mean thing to do in revenge for that slap.

"I'm sorry."

"Do you have an idea?" she asked me, coldly. "A plan?"

"No, I don't have a plan. I just want to find the guy who killed Sonia and Georges. And kill him."

"That's really stupid."

"Maybe it is. But it's the only way a piece of shit like that will get what he deserves."

"What I meant was, it's really stupid of you to risk your life." She rested her dark eyes on me, and there was a gentleness in them. "Unless you really are that unhappy."

13.

In which it's easier to explain things to other people than to understand them yourself

The fire sirens jolted me awake. The air coming in through the window smelled of burning. Hot, foul air. I learned later that the fire had started in a garbage dump in Septèmes-les-Vallons, a village just north of Marseilles. Not far from here, from George's apartment.

"They're tailing me," I'd said to Hélène Pessayre. "I'm sure of it. Sonia came back with me the other night. She slept in my house. All they had to do was follow her home. I was the one who led them to Mavros. Any time I go see a friend, sooner or later he's going to end up on their list."

We were still in Mavros's office. Trying to figure out a plan. To get me out of the fix I was in. The killer would call again this evening. He was expecting results. He wanted me to tell him where Babette was, or something similar. If I couldn't give him any assurances, he'd kill someone else. Maybe Fonfon or Honorine, if he didn't find one of my old party buddies to kill first.

"I'm stuck here," I'd lied to her. That was less than an hour ago. "I can't make a move without endangering the life of someone close to me."

She looked at me. I was starting to know those looks of hers. This one wasn't a completely trusting look. Her doubts persisted. "Actually, that's lucky for us."

"What is?"

"The fact that you can't make a move," she replied, with a touch of irony. "I mean, the fact that they have to tail you is their weak point."

I saw what she was getting at, and I didn't like it. "I don't follow you."

"Stop treating me like an idiot, Montale! You know perfectly well what I mean. They follow you, we'll be right behind them."

"And pounce on them at the first red light, is that it?"

I immediately regretted saying that. There was a veil of sadness over her eyes.

"I'm sorry, Hélène."

"Give me a cigarette."

I held out my pack. "Don't you ever buy any?"

"You always have some. And . . . we seem to be seeing a lot of each other, don't we?"

She said it without smiling, and her voice was weary.

"Montale," she continued softly, "we'll never get anywhere if you don't"—she took a long drag on her cigarette as she searched for the words—"if you don't believe in me. Not as a cop. As a woman. I thought you'd have understood that, after our conversation by the sea."

"What should I have understood?"

The words had slipped out. No sooner had I said them than they started echoing cruelly in my head. I'd said exactly the same thing to Lole, that terrible night when she'd told me it was all over. The years were passing, and I was still asking the same question. I still understood nothing about life. "The reason we keep coming back to the same place," I'd said to Mavros one night, after Pascale had left, "is because we're going around in circles. Because we're lost . . ." He'd nodded. He was going around in circles. He was lost. It's easier to explain these things to other people, I thought, than to understand them yourself.

Hélène Pessayre smiled just the way Lole had. Her answer was a little different. "Why don't you trust women? What have they done to you? Haven't they given you enough?

Have they disappointed you? They've made you suffer, is that it?"

Once again, she'd thrown me completely. "Maybe. Yes."

"Men have disappointed me too. They've made me suffer. Does that mean I have to hate all men?"

"I don't hate women."

"Let me tell you something, Montale. Sometimes, when you look at me, I feel as if I've been turned upside down. I feel all this emotion welling up in me."

"Hélène," I tried to interrupt her.

"Shut up, dammit! When you look at a woman, me or any woman, you go straight to the crux of things. But you also bring along your fears, your doubts, your anxieties, all the crap that's got your heart in a vise, all the things that make you say, 'It won't work, it'll never work.' Never the certainty that happiness is possible."

"What about you, do you believe in happiness?"

"I believe in genuine relationships between people. Between men and women. Without fear, which means without lies."

"Right. And where does that get us?"

"It gets us to this. Why are you so determined to kill that guy, that hitman?"

"Because of Sonia. And now because of Mavros."

"Mavros, I can understand. He was your friend. But Sonia? I already asked you if you loved her. Is that what you felt that night? That you loved her? You didn't answer. You just said you wanted to see her again."

"Yes, I wanted to see her. And . . ."

"And then maybe . . . perhaps . . . who knows? The usual things, right? And you set off to see her again, with part of you incapable of hearing what it was she wanted, what she was expecting of you. Have you ever really been able to give? To give everything to a woman?"

"Yes," I said, thinking how much I'd loved Lole.

Hélène Pessayre gave me a tender look. Like the other day on the terrace at Ange's, when she'd put her hand on mine. But she wasn't about to say, "I love you" any more than she had the last time. Or come and snuggle in my arms. I was sure of that.

"You may believe that, Montale. But I don't believe you. And that woman didn't believe it either. You didn't give her your trust. You didn't tell her you believed in her. You didn't show it either. Not enough, anyway."

"Why should I trust you?" I said. "Because that's what you're getting at, isn't it? That's what you're asking me. To trust you."

"Yes. For once in your life, Montale. Trust a woman. Trust me. And then I can trust you. If the two of us can figure out a plan, I want to be sure of you. I want to be sure of your reasons for killing that guy."

"You'd let me kill him?" I said, surprised. "Would you?"

"Yes, if what's driving you isn't hate, or despair, but love. The love you were starting to feel for Sonia. You know, I have very clear-cut views about things. And a strong sense of morality. But . . . Do you know how many years they gave Giovanni Brusca, the bloodiest of all Mafia hitmen?"

"I didn't even know he'd been arrested."

"A year ago. At home. He was eating spaghetti with his family. Twenty-six years. He's the man who blew up Judge Falcone."

"And murdered an eleven-year-old boy."

"Just twenty-six years. I wouldn't feel any remorse if that hitman of yours died, instead of having to stand trial. But . . . we're not there yet."

No, we weren't there yet. I got up. I could still hear the fire sirens, coming from all directions. The air was acrid, sickening. I closed the window. I'd been sleeping on Mavros's bed for the past half-hour. Hélène Pessayre and her team had left. And, with her agreement, I'd gone upstairs to Mavros's apartment, above the gym. I was supposed to wait there. Until another team arrived to see if it could spot the car of the guys who were following me. We were both sure they were there, right outside the door, or somewhere nearby.

"Do you have enough manpower to do that?"

"I'm dealing with two murders here."

"Have you mentioned the Mafia in your reports?"

"No, of course not."

"Why not?"

"Because I'm pretty sure I'd be taken off the case."

"You're taking a big risk."

"No. I know exactly what I'm getting into."

Mavros's apartment was exceptionally tidy. There was something almost morbid about it. Everything was the way it had been before Pascale left. She hadn't taken much with her when she'd gone. Just a few trifles. Some trinkets, things Mavros had given her. A few dishes. A few CDs, a few books. The TV. The new vacuum cleaner they'd just bought.

For a modest rent, some mutual friends of theirs, Jean and Bella, had let Pascale move into their little fully furnished house in a quiet corner of Marseilles, on Rue Villa-Paradis, at the top of Rue Breteuil. They'd just had their third child, and the house, which was on two floors but narrow, had become too small for them.

Pascale had immediately fallen in love with the house. The street still looked like a village street, and was likely to stay that way for many more years to come. Mavros didn't understand. "I'm not leaving you because of Benoît," she'd told him. "I'm leaving because of me. I need to rethink my life. Not ours. Mine. Maybe one day, I'll be able to think of you again the way I should, the way I used to."

Mavros had made this apartment a tomb for his memories. Even the bed, on which I'd collapsed in a state of total exhaustion, didn't seem to have been touched since Pascale had left. Now I understood why he'd been in such a hurry to find a girlfriend. It was so that he wouldn't have to sleep here.

The saddest thing in the apartment was in the toilet: a collage, behind glass, of all the best photos from their years together. I imagined Mavros watching his own failure parade in front of his eyes every time he took a leak. He should at least have taken that down, I thought.

I removed the glass and placed it carefully on the floor. There was one photo I was particularly fond of. Lole had taken it one summer, at the house of some friends in La Ciotat. Georges and Pascale were sleeping on a bench in the garden, with George's head resting on Pascale's shoulder. They exuded peace and happiness. Carefully, I peeled the photo loose and slipped it into my wallet.

The phone rang. It was Hélène Pessayre.

"It's done, Montale. My men are in place. They've spotted them. They're parked outside number 148. A blue Fiat Punto. There are two of them."

"Good," I said. I felt as if I were suffocating.

"So, are we sticking to what we said?"

"Yes."

I should have said more. But I'd just figured out a risk-free way to see Babette, without anyone else knowing. Even Hélène Pessayre.

"Montale?"

"Yes."

"Are you O.K.?"

"Sure. What's up with the firefighters?"

"A big forest fire. It started in Septèmes, but it seems to be spreading. They say another one's started near Plan-de-Cuques, but I don't know any more about that. The worst of it is that the tanker planes can't take off, because of the mistral."

"Shit," I said. I took a deep breath. "Hélène?"

"What?"

"Before I go home, the way we agreed, I . . . I need to drop in on an old friend."

"Who?" The doubt had crept back into her voice.

"This isn't a trick, Hélène. His name is Félix. He used to run a restaurant on Rue Caisserie. I promised I'd go see him. We often go fishing together. He lives in Vallon-des-Auffes. I have to go there before I go home."

"Why didn't you tell me this before?"

"I only just remembered."

"Call him."

"He doesn't have a phone. Since his wife died and he retired, he's preferred to be left alone. The only way to call him is to leave a message with the pizzeria next door." That much was true. "And he doesn't need to hear me, he needs to see me."

"Right." I seemed to hear her weighing the pros and the cons. "So what do we do?"

"I park in the garage of the Bourse Center. I go up to the mall, walk back out and grab a taxi. It'll take me an hour at the most."

"And what if they follow you?"

"I'll see."

"O.K."

"So long."

"Montale, if you find out anything about Babette Bellini's whereabouts, you won't forget me, will you?"

"I won't forget you, captain."

A thick column of black smoke rose above North Marseilles. The hot air was seeping into my lungs. If the mistral didn't die down, I thought, this could last for several days. Several nerve-racking days. So much forest and vegetation and even scrub burning was a tragedy for the region. People still had vivid memories of the terrible fire in August 1989, which had devastated eight thousand six hundred acres on the slopes of the Montagne Sainte-Victoire.

I went into the nearest bar and asked for a beer. The owner was listening intently to Radio France Provence, and so were all the customers. The fire was spreading. It had reached the area around the little village of Plan-de-Cuques, and they were starting to evacuate people from the more isolated villas.

I thought again about my plan to get Babette to a safe place. It was still feasible, on one condition: that the mistral die down. But the mistral could blow for a day, or three days, or six, or nine.

I finished my beer and asked for another. The die is cast, I thought. We'd soon see if I still had a future. If not, there was surely a place under the ground where Manu, Ugo, Mavros and I could have a nice quiet game of *belote*.

14.

IN WHICH WE LEARN THE EXACT MEANING OF THE EXPRESSION "A DEATHLY SILENCE"

I started my car. I knew they'd be following me. First the Mafia guys. Then the cops. In other circumstances, I might have found it amusing to be tailed. But I wasn't in the mood to be amused. I wasn't in the mood for anything. Just doing what I'd made up my mind to do. Without any scruples. Knowing me, the fewer scruples I had, the more chance I had of seeing my plan through.

I felt exhausted. Mavros's death had at last sunk in. It was as if his corpse had taken up residence in my body, as if I was its coffin. That hour's sleep had drained me of all the emotions that had overwhelmed me when I saw his face for the last time.

With a steady hand, Hélène Pessayre had uncovered the top of Mavros's face and pulled the sheet down to his chin. She had cast a furtive glance at me. It was just a formality, identifying him. Slowly, I'd leaned over George's body, tenderly stroked his graying hair with the tips of my fingers, and kissed his forehead.

"Goodbye, old friend," I'd said through gritted teeth.

Hélène Pessayre had taken me by the arm and led me quickly to the other side of the room. "Does he have any family?"

His mother, Angelika, had gone back to Nauplia, in the south of the Peloponnese, after her husband's death. His elder brother, Panayotis, had been living in New York for twenty years. Andreas, the youngest of the three brothers, lived in Fréjus. But Georges hadn't spoken to him in ten years. He and his wife, who had voted Socialist in '81, had switched to the PRP, and finally the National Front. As for Pascale, I didn't really want to call her. I didn't even know if

I still had her number. She'd dropped out of Mavros's life. Which meant she'd also dropped out of mine.

"No," I lied. "I was his only friend."

His last friend.

Now, there was no one left in Marseilles I could call. Of course, there were still quite a few people I liked, like Didier Perez and a few others. But there was no one to whom I could say, "You remember . . ." That was what friendship was, all the memories you had in common that you could put on the table with a nice sea bass grilled in fennel. Only the words "You remember . . ." make it possible to confide your most intimate thoughts, those regions of yourself you feel most embarrassed about. For years, I'd unloaded my doubts, my fears, my anxieties on Mavros, and he'd driven me crazy with the way he was so certain about everything, the way he had cut and dried opinions about everything. And after a few bottles of wine, depending on our mood, we'd usually come to the conclusion that, whatever your attitude to life, joy and sorrow were nothing but a lottery.

When I got to the Bourse Center, I did what I'd said I would. I managed to find a parking space without too much difficulty two levels underground, then took the escalator up to the mall. The air conditioning was a pleasant surprise. I could happily have spent the rest of the afternoon here. The place was crowded. The mistral had driven the people of Marseilles off the beaches, and they were killing time as best they could. Young guys especially. They could eye up the girls, and it cost less than a ticket for a movie.

I'd wagered on the fact that one of the two Mafiosi would follow me. I'd also wagered on the fact that he wouldn't be too happy to see me taking such an interest in the summer sales. So, after lingering for a while, looking at shirts and pants, I took the central escalator up to the second level.

There, a metal footbridge led across Rue Bir-Hakeim and Rue de Fabres. Then I took another escalator back down to the Canebière. All the while, acting as casual as possible.

The taxi stand was nearby. Five drivers were waiting by their cabs, desperate for customers.

"Did you see this?" the driver I chose asked, showing me his windshield.

It was covered with a fine layer of soot. That was when I noticed the flakes of ash coming down. The fire must be huge.

"Fucking fire," I said.

"And fucking mistral! The fire's spreading and no one can do anything. I don't know how many firefighters and rescue workers they've sent. Fifteen hundred, eighteen hundred . . . But it's coming from all directions now. They say it's even reached Allauch."

Allauch!

That was another village on the edge of Marseilles. A thousand people lived there. The fire was encroaching on the city's green belt, stripping the forest bare. There were other villages in its path. Simiane, Mimet . . .

"And of course, they're busy protecting people and houses . . ."

It was always the same story. The priority for the firefighters and the tanker planes—if and when they could fly—had to be the villas and the housing developments. But the question was why there weren't strict rules that builders had to follow. Heavy shutters. Nebulizers. Water tanks. Firebreaks. Quite often, the fire engines couldn't even get in between the houses and the front of the fire.

"What are they saying about the mistral?"

"It should die down during the night. Get weaker. I hope it's true."

"So do I," I said, thoughtfully.

The fire was ahead of me. Yes, but not only the fire.

*

"You can't be sure, Fabio," Félix said.

He'd been surprised to see me. Especially in the afternoon. I visited him every two weeks. Usually after leaving Fonfon's bar. We'd have an aperitif, and chat for a couple of hours. Céleste's death had really shaken him. At first, we thought he was going to let himself die. He didn't eat, and refused to go out. He didn't even want to go fishing, and that was really a bad sign.

Félix was only a Sunday fisherman. But he was part of the fishermen's community in Vallon-des-Auffes. They were all Italians, from around Rapallo, Santa Margarita and Maria del Campo. Along with Bernard Grandona and Gilbert Georgi, he was responsible for organizing the local fishermen's festival, the festival of Saint Pierre. Last year, Félix had taken me out in his boat to witness the ceremony from beyond the sea wall. The foghorn had blown, and flowers and petals had been strewn on the water in memory of those who'd died at sea.

Honorine—who'd known Céleste since they were children—and Fonfon took turns with me in keeping Félix company. At weekends, we'd invite him to dinner. I'd come and fetch him, and take him back home later. Then one Sunday morning, he arrived at my house by boat. He'd been fishing. It was a fine catch. Sea bream, rainbow wrasse, and even a few gray mullet.

"Dammit!" he laughed, as he climbed the steps to my terrace. "You haven't even gotten the barbecue started."

For me, that moment was more moving than the Saint Pierre festival. It was a celebration of life over death. Of course, we drank to that, and for the umpteenth time Félix told us how, when his grandfather wanted to get married, he'd gone all the way to Rapallo to find a wife. Before he'd even finished, Fonfon, Honorine and I cried in unison, "And by boat, if you please!"

He looked at us in surprise. "I'm rambling, aren't I?"

"No, Félix," Honorine replied. "You're not rambling. You can tell us your memories a hundred times. They're the most beautiful things in your life. And they're even better when they're shared."

And they started in on their own memories. The afternoon flew by, helped along by several bottles of white wine from Cassis. Fontcreuse, which I always kept for the good times. Then, inevitably, we'd talked about Manu and Ugo. We'd been going to Félix's restaurant since we were fifteen. Félix and Céleste would feed us on *fegatelli* pizzas, spaghetti *alle vongole*, and lasagne made with goat's cheese. It was there that we'd learned, once and for all, what a real bouillabaisse was like. When it came to bouillabaisse, even Honorine didn't come close to her friend Céleste. And it was as he was coming out of Félix's restaurant that Manu had been shot down, five years ago. But we always stopped our reminiscences before that point. Ugo and Manu were still alive. They just weren't with us, that was all, and we missed them. Like Lole.

Félix had started singing "Maruzzella," my father's favourite song. We sang the chorus in unison, and we all wept for the people we loved who weren't with us anymore. *Maruzzella, o Maruzzella . . .*

Félix looked at me. In his eyes I could see the same fear Fonfon and Honorine had when they knew I was in deep shit. He was at his window when I arrived, looking out to sea, his collection of *Pieds-Nickelés* comics beside him on the table. That was all he ever read, and he reread them endlessly. And as time passed, he'd grown increasingly to look like one of the characters, Ribouldingue, minus the beard.

We talked about the fire. A fine ash was falling on Vallon-des-Auffes too. And Félix confirmed that the fire had moved toward Allauch. He'd just heard the commander of the regional fire department on the news, saying we were racing headlong into disaster.

He brought out two beers. "Are you in trouble?" he asked.

"Yes," I replied. "Serious trouble."

And I told him the whole story.

Félix knew something about gangsters, and the Mafia. An uncle of his, on his mother's side, a guy named Charles Sartène, had been a strong-arm man for Mémé Guérini, the undisputed head of the Marseilles underworld after the war. Gradually, I led up to the deaths of Sonia and Mavros. When I said that Fonfon and Honorine were at the top of the list of possible targets, I had the impression that the lines on his face became even more deeply etched.

Then I told him how I got here, the precautions I'd taken to give the killers the slip. He shrugged. His eyes moved away from mine and lingered idly on the little harbor of Vallon-des-Auffes. It was a long way from the hustle and bustle of the world. A haven of peace. Like Les Goudes. One of those places where Marseilles exists in the imagination of those who gaze at her.

I remembered some lines by Louis Brauquier:

> *I am walking toward the people of my silence*
> *Slowly, toward those I can be silent with;*
> *I shall come from afar, enter and then sit down*
> *I am coming to find what I shall need to leave again.*

Félix turned to look at me again. His eyes were slightly misty, as if he had been crying inside. He made no comment, just asked, "Where do I fit into all this?"

"I got this idea in my head that the safest way to meet Babette is at sea. These guys are outside my front door. If I take the boat out at night, they're not going to follow me.

They'll wait for me to come back. That's what happened the other night."

"Right."

"I'll tell Babette to come here. You can take her over to Frioul, and I'll meet the two of you there. I'll bring something to eat and drink."

"Do you think she'll agree?"

"To come?"

"No, to what you're thinking of. Drop the idea of publishing her report . . . All those things that'll implicate people."

"I don't know."

"It won't make any difference. They'll kill her anyway. And you too, I suppose. People like that . . ."

Félix had never been able to understand how someone could become a professional killer. He'd often talked to me about his relationship with Charles Sartène. Everyone in the family called him Uncle. A great guy. Kind. Considerate. Félix had wonderful memories of family gatherings, with Uncle at the head of the table. Always very well dressed. The children would come and sit on his lap. One day, a few years before he died, talking to Antoine, one of his nephews, who wanted to become a journalist, Uncle had said, "If only I was younger! I'd go along to the offices of *Le Provençal*, kill one or two of the guys on the top floor for you, and you'd see, boy, they'd hire you straight away."

Everyone had laughed. Félix, who must have been about nineteen at the time, had never forgotten those words. Or the laughter. He'd refused to go to Uncle's funeral, and had broken with his family for good. He'd never regretted it.

"I know, Félix," I said. "But I have to take the risk. Once I've talked to Babette, I'll see." Then, to reassure him, I said, "And I won't be acting alone. There's this cop I've been talking to . . ."

There was fear mixed with anger in his eyes. "You mean you talked to the cops?"

"Not the cops. One cop. A woman. The woman who's investigating the deaths of Sonia and Mavros."

He shrugged, as he had earlier. A little more wearily, maybe. "If the cops are involved, Fabio, count me out. It complicates everything. And increases the risks. Shit, you know what it's like here . . ."

"Wait, Félix. This is me you're talking to, right? If I do bring in the cops, it won't be till later. After I've seen Babette. After we've decided what to do with the papers. This woman, this police captain, doesn't even know Babette is coming. She's in the same position as the killers. She's waiting. They're all waiting for me to find Babette."

"O.K.," he said. He looked out the window again. The flakes of ash were coming down more thickly now. "It hasn't snowed here for years. Instead, we have this. Fucking fire."

He looked back at me, then down at the copy of *Les Pieds Nickelés* open in front of him. "O.K.," he repeated. "But this fucking mistral has to stop first, or we won't be able to go out."

"I know."

"Couldn't you see her here?"

"No, Félix. That trick I pulled in the Bourse Center was a one-off. I couldn't try anything like that again. They'll be suspicious now. And I don't want that. I need them to trust me."

"Trust you? Are you serious?"

"O.K., not trust exactly. You know what I mean, Félix. I need them to think I'm playing fair. That I'm just a poor shmuck who doesn't know anything."

"All right," he said, thoughtfully. "Tell Babette to come. She can stay here. Until the mistral dies down. As soon as we can put to sea, I'll call Fonfon."

"You can call me."

"No, not at your house. I'll call Fonfon. At his bar. O.K., tell Babette I'll be here. She can come whenever she wants."

I stood up. So did he. I put my arm around his shoulder and hugged him.

"It'll be all right," he muttered. "We'll sort it out, huh? We've always sorted things out."

"I know."

I kept hugging him, and he made no move to free himself. He knew there was something else I still had to ask him. I imagined his stomach tensing at the thought of it. Mine certainly was.

"Félix," I said. "Do you still have Manu's gun?"

The smell of death filled the room. I understood the exact meaning of the expression "a deathly silence."

"I need it, Félix."

15.

IN WHICH THE IMMINENCE OF AN EVENT
CREATES A KIND OF BLACK HOLE

They phoned one after the other. First Hélène Pessayre, then the killer. I'd phoned Babette before that. But from Fonfon's. When Félix had said he'd call Fonfon's and not my house, he'd started me thinking. He was right, my phone might be tapped. Hélène Pessayre was perfectly capable of something like that. And if the cops were listening in on my calls, then anything I said might end up in the ears of a mafioso. You just had to pay, as Fargette had done for years. You just had to agree on a price. And for the guys camped outside my door, the price was unlikely to be a problem.

I'd looked out and tried to spot them on the street. The killers, and the cops. But I couldn't see any Fiat Punto or any Renault 21. It didn't matter. They had to be there. Somewhere.

"Can I use your phone?" I'd said to Fonfon as I walked in.

The only thing that mattered right now was to see my plan through. Even though what happened after I found Babette and talked to her was still a complete blank. The imminence of her arrival created a kind of black hole that was sucking me into it.

"There you go," Fonfon grunted, putting the phone on the bar counter. "It's like the post office here, but the calls are free, and you get a *pastis* thrown in."

"Hold on, Fonfon!" I cried, dialing Bruno's number in the Cévennes.

"I mean, you come and go like the wind. Faster than the mistral. And when you're here, you don't say anything. You don't explain. The only thing we know is that wherever you go, you leave a trail of corpses behind you. Goddammit, Fabio!"

Slowly, I put down the receiver. Fonfon had poured *pastis* into two small glasses. He placed one of them in front of me, clinked his glass against mine, and drank without waiting for me.

"The less you know—" I began.

He exploded. "No way! Don't give me that bullshit! Not now. That's over! You explain yourself, Fabio! I saw the face of the guy in the Fiat Punto. As close as I'm seeing you now. We passed each other. He was on his way to Michel's to buy cigarettes. He looked at me."

"A Mafia guy."

"Sure . . . But I mean, I recognized his face. I'd seen it not long ago."

"What? Here?"

"No. In the newspaper. His photo was there."

"In the newspaper?"

"Fabio, when you read the newspaper, don't you ever look at the pictures?"

"Yes, of course."

"Well, his photo was there. Ricardo Bruscati. Richie, to his friends. They mentioned him when that book about Yann Piat came out."

"What did they say about him? Do you remember?"

He shrugged. "What do I know? You should ask Babette, she'll know." He looked me straight in the eyes when he said that.

"What made you mention Babette?"

"Because this whole mess is all down to her, isn't it? Honorine found the note that came with the disks. You left it on the table. So she read it."

Fonfon's eyes were shining with anger. I'd never seen him like this before. Screaming and cursing, sure. But that anger in his eyes, never.

He leaned toward me. "Fabio," he said. His voice was a little softer, but firm. "If there was only me . . . I don't give a damn, you know. But there's Honorine. I don't want anything to happen to her. Do you understand?"

I felt a wrench in my stomach. So much love.

All I could find to say was "Give me another drink."

"I'm not being nasty or anything. What Babette does is her business. And you're big enough to fuck up whichever way you like. I'm not going to dictate to you what you can and can't do. But if those guys touch a hair on Honorine's head . . ."

He didn't finish the sentence. But his eyes told me what he couldn't say in words: that he was holding me responsible for whatever happened to Honorine. Just to her.

"Nothing will happen to her. I swear. Or to you."

"Right," he said, not really convinced.

But we clinked glasses all the same. For real, this time.

"I swear," I repeated.

"O.K., let's drop it," he said.

"No, let's not drop it. I'll call Babette, and then I'll tell you what she says."

Babette agreed. She'd come, and we'd talk. My plan suited her. But, from the tone of her voice, I guessed it wouldn't be a piece of cake, getting her to give up on publishing her report. We didn't pursue that for now. The important thing was to talk about it face to face.

"I have some new information," Hélène Pessayre said.

"So have I," I replied. "You first."

"My men have identified one of the guys."

"So have I. Ricardo Bruscati."

Silence at the other end.

"Impressed, huh?" I said, amused.

"Quite impressed."

"I used to be a cop, too."

I tried to imagine her face at that moment. The look of disappointment on it. I didn't suppose Hélène Pessayre liked anyone beating her to the draw.

"Hélène?"

"Yes, Montale."

"Don't make that face!"

"What are you talking about?"

"I found out about Ricardo Bruscati by chance. My neighbor, Fonfon, recognized him. He'd seen his photo recently in the newspaper. That's all I know about him. So go on."

She cleared her throat. She was still a little angry. "It doesn't make our job any easier."

"What doesn't?"

"The fact that the second man is Bruscati."

"Why not? Now we know who we're dealing with, don't we?"

"No. Bruscati is from the Var. He's not known for slicing people up with knives. He's a strong-arm man who settles scores. Just that, nothing else."

My turn to fall silent. I saw what she was getting at. "There's another man. Is that what you're telling me? A real Mafia hitman?"

"Yes."

"Who's probably having a quiet aperitif on the terrace of the New York as we speak."

"Precisely. And the fact that they also hired Bruscati, who isn't just anybody, shows they mean business."

"Was Bruscati mixed up in the murder of Yann Piat?"

"Not as far as I know. In fact, I very much doubt it. But he was one of the people who broke up Yann Piat's big meeting at L'Espace 3000 in Fréjus on March 16th 1993. You remember?"

"Yes. They used tear gas. It was Fargette who gave the orders. Yann Piat didn't fit in with his political plans."

I'd read about it in the papers.

"Fargette was still backing the UDF candidate," she went on. "With the approval of the National Front. I think Bruscati's still working for the National Front behind the scenes, handling security for them between Marseilles and Nice, recruiting people, training them . . . There's a file on all that on the white disk."

I'd skimmed through that file. It didn't tell me anything I hadn't gleaned from reading the newspapers. It was more like a summary of the situation in the Var than an explosive document. But I'd lingered for a while over the links between Fargette and the National Front. I remembered part of the transcript of a phone conversation between the Marseilles gang boss Daniel Savastano and Fargette. *There are people who want to work, who want to get the city back on track. I told him, if you have friends who have businesses, that kind of thing, let's try putting them to work . . .*"

"Did Bruscati kill Fargette?"

Fargette had been killed the day after the meeting, at his home in Italy.

"Fargette was killed by four men."

"Yes, I know. But . . ."

"What's the point of speculating? It's quite possible that after the murder of Yann Piat, Bruscati killed a whole lot of people. People who stood in their way."

"For instance?"

"For instance, Michel Régnier."

I whistled through my teeth. After Fargette's death, Régnier had been considered the godfather of the South of France. The godfather of the local underworld, not the Mafia. On September 30th 1996—his birthday—he'd been riddled with bullets, with his wife looking on.

"To me, the fact that Bruscati is here now means one thing, and one thing only: he's working for the Mafia. And that means the Mafia's really taken economic control of the region.

I think that's one of the ideas in your friend's report, and it puts an end to all the speculation about a gangland war."

"Economic control, not political control?"

"I haven't yet dared to open the black disk."

"Right. The less we know . . ." I said again, mechanically.

"Do you seriously think that?"

It was as if I was hearing Babette.

"I don't think anything, Hélène. All I'm saying is that some people are dead and some are alive. And among the ones who are alive, there are some who were responsible for the others being dead. And most of them are still at large. And still doing business. Yesterday with the Var and Marseilles underworld, today with the Mafia. Do you follow me?"

She didn't reply. I heard her light a cigarette. "Any news about your friend Babette Bellini?"

"I think I've finally located her," I lied, in a confident voice.

"Well, I'm patient, even if they aren't. I'll wait for your call . . . By the way, Montale, I changed the team after you left the Bourse Center. As you were on your way home, we didn't want to risk being spotted. It's a white Peugeot 304 now."

"Which reminds me," I said. "I have a favor to ask you."

"Go on."

"As you have the manpower, I'd like a twenty-four-hour watch to be kept on Honorine's house and Fonfon's bar, which is very near."

Silence.

"I'll have to think about it."

"Hélène, I'm not going to blackmail you. 'I'll give you this if you give me that'—that's not my style. But if anything goes wrong . . . I don't want to have to kiss the corpses of those two, Hélène. I love them more than anything else in my life. They're the only ones I have left, you understand?"

I closed my eyes to think about Fonfon and Honorine, and saw Lole's face. I loved her more than anything else in my life too. She wasn't my woman anymore. She was living far away, with another man. But like Fonfon and Honorine, she still gave me what no one else could. A sense of what love was.

"All right," Hélène Pessayre said. "But not before tomorrow morning."

"Thanks."

I was about to hang up.

"Montale."

"Yes?"

"I hope we'll get this whole mess over with very soon. And that . . . that we'll come out of it as friends. I mean . . . that you'll want to invite me to your house, to have dinner with Honorine and Fonfon."

"I hope so, Hélène. I really do. It'd give me great pleasure to invite you to my house."

"Take care of yourself in the meantime."

And she hung up. Too quickly. I had time to hear the small whistling sound that followed. My phone was being tapped. The bitch! I thought, but I didn't have time to think anything else, or even to savor her last words, because the phone rang again. And I knew the next voice I heard wouldn't be anywhere near as disturbing as Hélène Pessayre's.

"Any news, Montale?"

I'd decided to keep things low key. No clever remarks. No wisecracks. I'd toe the line, pretend I was on my knees, a poor idiot at the end of his tether.

"Yes, I spoke to Babette on the phone."

"Good. Is that who you were just talking to?"

"No, I was just talking to the cops. I can't get them off my back. Two friends of mine dead, they find that hard to swallow. They've been giving me the third degree."

"Well, that's your problem. When did you phone the shit stirrer? When you got away from us this afternoon?"

"That's right."

"You're sure she's not here, in Marseilles?"

"I'm being straight with you. She can be here in two days."

He paused for a moment. "Two days, Montale, that's all I'm giving you. I have another name on my list. And that pretty captain of yours won't like it one little bit."

"O.K. What do we do when she's here?"

"I'll let you know. And Montale, tell the Bellini woman not to come empty-handed. She has some things of ours that we'd like to get back."

"I already mentioned it to her."

"Good. You're making progress."

"What about the rest of it? Her report?"

"We don't give a fuck about that. She can write whatever she wants, wherever she wants. It'll be like pissing in the wind. It always is." He laughed, then his voice again became as sharp as the knife he handled so skillfully. "Two days."

They were only interested in the contents of the black disk. The one neither Hélène Pessayre nor I dared look at. In her draft report, Babette had written: *The money laundering networks are still in place, and in this region they are controlled by 'boards of directors' that bring together influential politicians, businessmen and local representatives of the Mafia.* She mentioned a number of "mixed companies" created by the Mafia and run by prominent businessmen.

"One more thing, Montale. Don't pull this afternoon's stunt again. O.K.?"

"You got it."

I let him hang up. There was the same whistling sound. I needed a *pastis* badly. And a little music. An old Nat King Cole track. "The Lonesome Road," with Anita O'Day as guest star. Yes, that was what I needed before joining Fonfon and Honorine. We were supposed to be having vegetable *farcis*. The taste of courgettes, tomatoes and eggplants, I knew, would keep death at bay. This evening more than ever, I needed those two around me.

16.

In which the game is being played, unwittingly, on the devil's chess board

It was while we were eating that I started to have my doubts.

The *farcis* were delicious, of course. Honorine, I had to admit, had a wonderful knack for making sure the meat and vegetables stayed tender. That was what made her *farcis* so different than the ones you found in restaurants, in which the meat was always a little too crunchy on the outside. Except perhaps at the Sud du Haut, a little restaurant on Cours Julien that still specialized in family-style cooking.

But as I ate, I couldn't stop thinking about the situation I was in. For the first time, I had two killers and two cops outside my door. Good and Evil allowed to park in front of my house. A stalemate. With me in the middle. Like the spark that could set off the powder keg. Was that the spark I'd been dreaming of since Lole left? To make my death a last spark? I started sweating. Even if Babette and I managed to avoid getting out throats cut by the hitman, I told myself, we'd still have Bruscati's bullets to dodge.

"More?" Honorine asked.

We were eating inside, because of the mistral. It had dropped a little, but was still blowing quite strongly. According to the news, the fire was spreading all around Marseilles. In one day, nearly five thousand acres of Aleppo pines and scrubland had gone up in smoke. It was a tragedy. Trees that had been planted only twenty-five years ago as part of a reforestation program were gone. Everything would have to be started all over again. People were already talking of a collective trauma. And the debate was in full swing. Should there be a twelve-mile buffer zone of almond trees, olives and vines between the edge of the Etoile massif and the Marseilles area? Yes, but who would pay? In this society, you always had to think of the bottom line. Even in the worst situations, money came first.

By the time we got to the cheese, we were running low on wine and Fonfon suggested going to his bar to get some.

"I'll go," I said.

Something wasn't right, and I wanted to make sure. Even if the answer turned out to be something I didn't like. I found it hard to believe that Hélène Pessayre had had my phone tapped. Of course, I knew she was capable of it, but it didn't fit in with what she'd said before she hung up. About our being friends when it was over. Above all, a professional like her would never have hung up first.

In Fonfon's bar, I dialed Hélène Pessayre's cellphone.

"Yes?" she said.

Music in the background. An Italian singer.

un po' di là del mare c'è una terra chiara
che di confini e argini non sa

"Montale here. I hope I'm not disturbing you?"

un po' di là del mare c'è una terra chiara

"I'm just out of the shower."

Instantly, images—carnal, sensual images—unreeled in front of my eyes. For the first time, I caught myself thinking of Hélène Pessayre with desire. I wasn't immune to her charms, of course—far from it—but our relationship was so complex, so tense at times, there was no room for feelings. At least, that's what I'd thought. Until now. My cock was responding to these fleeting images. I smiled. It was a pleasure to know I could still get a hard-on at the thought of a woman's body.

"Montale?"

I've never been a voyeur, but I used to love it when I caught Lole coming out of the shower, taking a towel, and wrapping herself in it, leaving only her wet legs and shoulders bare. As soon as I heard the water stop running, I always found something to do in the bathroom. I'd wait until she lifted her hair onto the back of her neck and then go to her. I think that was when I desired her the most, no matter what time it was. I loved her smile, when our eyes met in the mirror. And the shudder that went through her when I kissed her neck. Lole.

un po' di là del mare c'è una terra sincera

"Yes," I said, trying to get my thoughts—and my cock— under control. "I have a question to ask you."

"It had better be important," she replied, with a laugh. "Seeing what time it is."

She turned down the volume.

"This is serious, Hélène. Did you have my phone tapped?"

"What?"

I had my answer. It wasn't her.

"Hélène, my phone is being tapped."

"Since when?"

A shudder went down my spine. I hadn't even thought about that. Since when? If it was since this morning, then Babette, Bruno and his family were in danger.

"I don't know. I didn't realize until tonight, after you called."

After I'd called Babette, who'd hung up first, her or me? I couldn't remember. But I had to. The second time, it was me. The first time . . . The first time, it was her. "Go to hell!" she'd said. No, there hadn't been that characteristic whistling sound afterwards. I was sure of it. But could I be sure of myself? Really sure? No. I had to call Le Castellas. Immediately.

"Did you phone your friend Babette Bellini from your house tonight?"

"No. This morning. Hélène, who's behind these phone taps?"

"You didn't tell me you knew where she was."

The woman was implacable. Even naked and wrapped in a bath towel.

"I told you I'd located her."

"And where is she?"

"In the Cévennes. I'm trying to persuade her to come to Marseilles. Shit, Hélène, this is serious!" I'd raised my voice.

"Stop getting worked up when you're caught out, Montale! We could have gotten up there in three hours!"

"So there would have been what?" I cried. "A procession of cars? Yes, of course! You, me, the killers, other cops, other killers . . . One following the other, like after I left Mavros's gym this afternoon!"

She didn't reply.

"Hélène," I said, more calmly, "it's not that I don't trust you. But you can't be sure of anything or anyone. Your superiors. The cops in your team. The proof of it is—"

"But this is *me*, dammit, this is *me*!" She was the one yelling now. "You could have told *me*, couldn't you?"

I closed my eyes. The images in my head weren't of Hélène Pessayre coming out of the shower anymore, but of the captain who'd given me a slap this morning.

I wasn't getting anywhere, she was right.

"You haven't answered my question. Who among your people could have done it?"

"I don't know," she said, calmer now. "I don't know."

There was a heavy silence.

"Who's the singer I heard?" I asked, to relieve the tension.

"Gianmaria Testa," she replied wearily. "Good, isn't he?" Then, quite resolutely, "Montale, I'm coming over."

"People will talk," I said as a joke.

"Would you prefer it if I summoned you to Headquarters?"

I put down two liters of red wine from the estate of Villeneuve Flayosc, in Roquefort-la-Bédoule. A wine a Breton friend named Michel had introduced us to the previous winter. Château-les-mûres. Really delicious.

"He was nearly dying of thirst," Honorine said.

It was her way of saying I'd taken my time.

"Did you get lost in the cellar?" Fonfon chimed in.

I filled their glasses, then mine. "I had to make a phone call." And before they could make any comment on that, I said, "My phone's being tapped. The cops. I had to call Babette back."

Babette had left that afternoon, Bruno had told me. To stay with some friends of theirs in Nîmes. She was supposed to be taking the train for Marseilles late tomorrow morning.

"Why don't you take a vacation, Bruno? You and your family. Go away for a while."

I thought of Mavros. I'd told him exactly the same thing. Bruno answered in almost identical terms. Everyone thought they were stronger than Evil. As if Evil was a strange illness. But it was eating us all up, piece by piece.

"I have too many animals to take care of . . ."

"Shit, Bruno, your wife and children at least. These guys will stop at nothing."

"I know. But my friends and I control all the approaches to the mountain." He paused. "And we're armed."

May '68 against the Mafia. I could just see it in my head, and it made my blood run cold.

"Bruno," I said, "we don't know each other. I feel affection for you. Because of what you did for Babette. Taking her in, knowing the risks—"

He cut me off. "There's no danger. If you knew—"

He was starting to get on my nerves, him and his fail-safe security system. "Fuck it, Bruno! This is the Mafia we're talking about!"

I guess I was bugging him too, because he cut short our conversation. "O.K., Montale. I'll think about it. Thanks for calling."

Fonfon emptied his glass slowly. "I thought that woman trusted you. That captain."

"It wasn't her. She doesn't even know who gave the order."

"Ah," he said simply.

I could sense how worried he was. He looked for a long time at Honorine. She'd been unusually silent this evening. She was worried too. But about me, I knew. I was the last. The last of the three. The last survivor of the boys she'd seen growing up, the boys she'd loved like a mother. Manu and Ugo had been swallowed up by all that shit. She wouldn't survive if I went too. I knew that.

"But what's the story with Babette?" Honorine finally asked.

"It's a Mafia story," I said. "We know how it starts, but we don't know how it's going to end."

"Is it something to do with all those gangland killings they keep talking about on TV?"

"Yes, more or less."

Since Fargette's death, there'd been a bloodbath. As Hélène had said, Bruscati was almost certainly involved. I could remember the macabre list clearly. There had been Henri Diana, killed at point blank range in October '93. Noël

Dotori, shot down in October '94. José Ordioni, in December '94. Then in '96, Fargette's loyal lieutenants Michel Régnier and Jackie Champourlier. The latest on the list were Patrice Meillan and Jean-Charles Taran, one of the last "big names" in the Var underworld.

"For a long time, we've downplayed the activities of the Mafia in France," I said. "People only talked about the local underworld. Easier to think all these killings were part of a gang war. But now the Mafia's here. And it's taking over. Economically and . . . politically, too."

There was no need to look into the black disk to understand that. As Babette had written: *The new international financial environment is fertile ground for the criminalization of political life. Powerful but clandestine pressure groups linked to organized crime are springing up. In short, the crime syndicates are exerting their influence on national economic policies.*

In those countries that have recently switched to a market economy, and therefore of course in the European Union, key figures in politics and even in government have forged ties of allegiance to organized crime. The nature of the State is being transformed, as are the social structures. In the European Union, this situation is far from being limited to Italy, where the Mafia has penetrated the highest echelons of the State . . .

And when Babette turned her attention specifically to France, her prognosis was terrifying. The first shots had already been fired in the war against the legally constituted State, a war supported by politicians and industrialists. As the financial stakes were so enormous, it would be a war without mercy. *Yesterday, she wrote, a deputy who was in the way was killed. Tomorrow, it may be the turn of a major political figure: a prefect, or a minister. Today, everything is possible.*

"We're nothing to them. Just pawns."

Fonfon kept looking at me, gravely. Then he looked again at Honorine. For the first time, I saw them as they were. Old and tired. Older and more tired than ever. I wished none of this existed. But it did exist. And we found ourselves, unwittingly, on the Devil's chessboard. But maybe we'd always been there. It was pure chance, coincidence, that had made us realize it. Babette was that chance, that coincidence. And we were pawns. In a game being played to the death.

Sonia. Georges.

How to put an end to all of that?

Babette quoted a United Nations report: *Giving more powers to international law enforcement agencies is merely a palliative. Without simultaneous progress in economic and social development, organized crime will persist on a widespread and highly structured scale.*

How could we get out of this mess? Fonfon, Honorine, Babette and I?

"Would you like some more cheese? Is the *provolone* good?"

"Yes, Honorine, it's delicious. But . . ."

"Go on," Fonfon said, his voice falsely cheerful. "Just a little, so we can have another drink."

He poured me another glass without waiting to be asked.

I didn't believe in chance. Or coincidence. They are simply a sign that we've passed over to the other side of reality. Where there can be no compromise with the intolerable. Where one person's thoughts connect with another's. The way they do in love. Or in despair. That was why Babette had turned to me. Because I was ready to listen to her. I couldn't tolerate the intolerable.

17.

IN WHICH IT IS SAID THAT REVENGE GETS YOU NOWHERE, AND NEITHER DOES PESSIMISM

I was lost in thought. And my thoughts, as so often, were completely confused. Alcohol-induced, of course. I'd already drunk two big glasses of Lagavulin. The first one I almost downed in one go, as soon as I got back to my little cottage.

The images of Sonia were fading fast. As if she'd been only a dream. Barely three days. The warmth of her thigh against mine, her smile. These meager memories were fraying at the edges. Even her gray-blue eyes were fading. I was losing her. And Lole was again laying siege to my head. Where she belonged. Her long, thin fingers seemed to be unpacking the cases of our life together. The years gone by started again to dance in front of my eyes. Lole was dancing. Dancing for me.

I was sitting on the couch. She had put on "Amor Verdadero" by Ruben Gonzalez. Her eyes closed, her right hand lightly touching her stomach, her left hand raised, she barely moved. Only her hips swayed, setting her body in motion. Her whole body. Her beauty took my breath away.

Later, on this same couch, she snuggled in my arms, and I breathed in the smell of her moist skin and the heat of her solid but fragile body. We were overwhelmed with emotion. It was the time for short sentences. "I love you . . . I feel good here, you know . . . I'm happy . . . How about you?"

Ruben Gonzalez's album continued. "Alto Songo," "Los Sitio' Asere," "Pio Mentiroso . . ."

Months, weeks, days. Until you start hesitating, searching for words, and the sentences grow longer. "What I want is to . . . to keep you in my heart. I never want to lose you, not completely. My one wish is that we stay close, that we continue loving each other . . ."

The days and the last nights. "I still have a big place in my heart for you. There will always be a big place for you in my life . . ."

Lole. Her last words. "Don't let yourself go, Fabio."

And now death was hovering. As close to me as it was possible to be. And its smell was ever-present. The only perfume left to keep me company at night. The smell of death.

I emptied my glass, with my eyes closed. Enzo's face. His gray-blue eyes. Sonia's eyes. And Enzo's tears. If I had to kill that son of a bitch, it would be for him. Not for Sonia. Not even for Mavros. No. I realized it now. It would be for that boy, and only for him. For all the things you don't understand at that age. Death. Separation. Absence. That primal injustice, the absence of the father, the mother.

Enzo. Enzo, my boy.

What was the point of tears if they couldn't find their reason for being in another person's heart? Or in my own?

I had just refilled my glass when Hélène Pessayre knocked at my door. I'd almost forgotten she was supposed to be coming. It was nearly midnight.

There was a slightly awkward moment when we hesitated between shaking hands and embracing. We did neither, and I let her in.

"Come in," I said.

"Thanks."

We were both suddenly embarrassed.

"I won't show you around, it's too small."

"Bigger than my place, from what I can see. Here." She handed me a CD. Gianmaria Testa. *Extra-Muros*. "Now you can hear the whole of it."

I almost replied, "If I'd wanted to do that, I could have come over to your place."

"Thanks," I said. "Now, you'll have to come here to listen to it."

She smiled. I was talking nonsense.

"Would you like a drink?" I asked, showing her mine.

"I'd prefer wine."

I opened a bottle of Tempier '92, and poured her a glass. We clinked glasses and drank in silence. We hardly dared look at each other.

She was wearing stonewashed jeans and a dark blue denim shirt partly open over a white T-shirt. I was starting to be intrigued by the fact that I never saw her in a skirt or a dress. Maybe she doesn't like her legs, I thought.

Mavros had had a theory about that. "All women like showing their legs, even if their legs aren't as good as a model's or a movie star's. It's all part of the game of seduction. You know what I'm saying?"

"Sure."

He'd noticed that ever since Pascale had met Benoît at that party at Pierre and Marie's, she'd been wearing only pants.

"And yet she's still buying pantyhose. Even the ones that only come up to the thigh."

One morning, he'd felt so bad, he'd even searched through Pascale's latest purchases. They'd been living together in an uneasy truce for several weeks, waiting for Bella and Jean to move out of the little house on Rue Villa-Paradis. The previous evening, Pascale had told him she would be away for the weekend. When she'd left to join Benoît, she'd been wearing jeans, but Mavros knew that in her little traveling bag, she had miniskirts, pantyhose. Even the ones that only come up to the thigh.

"Just imagine that, Fabio," he'd said.

Barely half an hour after Pascale left, that Friday night, he'd called me, in despair.

I'd responded to his words with a sad smile. I didn't have any theories as to why a woman might put on a skirt in the morning, rather than a pair of pants. But when the time came, Lole did exactly the same, as I realized with some bitterness. During our last months together, she only ever wore jeans. And of course, the bathroom door was always closed when she came out of the shower.

I felt like asking Hélène Pessayre about it. But I thought it was maybe a little too bold. And besides, there was a grave look in her eyes now.

She took a pack of cigarettes from her bag and offered me one. "You see, I bought some."

For a while, we were both silent, wreathed in smoke.

"My father was killed eight years ago," she began, in a low voice. "I'd just finished my law studies. I wanted to be a lawyer."

"Why are you telling me this?"

"You asked me the other day if that was the way I spent my life. You remember? Dealing with all this shit. Wearing out my eyes on corpses . . ."

"I was angry. Anger is my defense mechanism. So is being vulgar."

"He was an examining magistrate. He'd worked on a lot of corruption cases. False invoices. The covert financing of political parties. One case took him a lot farther than he'd planned to go. He followed the trail from the undeclared funds of a political party—I won't say which, but it used to be the majority—all the way to a Panamanian bank called the Xoilan Trades. One of General Noriega's banks. Specializing in drug money."

Slowly, she told me the story. In her solemn, almost gravelly voice. One day, her father was informed by the Fraud Squad in Paris that Pierre-Jean Raymond, this political party's Swiss banker, was arriving in France. He immediately issued a summons against him. Raymond's briefcase was found to be full of very compromising documents. A minister and several members of parliament were implicated. Raymond was taken into custody. "They put me in with a bunch of Islamists," he would later complain to his political friends. "I didn't sleep a wink."

"My father indicted him for violation of the rules on the financing of political parties, misuse of social property, breach of trust, forgery and the use of forgeries. He was the first Swiss banker to be prosecuted in France in a case with political connections.

"My father could have stopped there. But he decided to follow up the financial connections. And that was when things got out of hand. Raymond also handled accounts for Spanish and Libyan clients as well as General Mobutu's real estate holdings, which have since been sold. In addition, he owned a casino in Switzerland on behalf of a group in Bordeaux, and managed about fifty Panamanian companies on behalf of Swiss, French and Italian firms . . ."

"The perfect set-up."

"Your friend Babette has gone where my father couldn't go. Right to the heart of the machine. Before coming here, I reread a few passages of her draft report. She uses the South of France as an example, but what she says holds true for the whole of the European Union. I was particularly struck by the terrible contradiction she points out: that the less united the States that signed up to Maastricht are against the Mafia, the more the Mafia flourishes on the dung heap—that's the term she uses—of obsolete and incompatible national laws."

"Yes," I said, "I read that too."

I'd almost talked about this earlier to Fonfon and Honorine. But then I'd told myself they'd already heard enough. It didn't tell them anything new about the mess Babette was in—the mess I was in too.

Babette backed up her comments with statements by leading European officials. *"What makes this failure of the Maastricht signatories all the more serious,"* Diemut Theato, chairman of the European Parliament's budget control committee, asserted, *"is that greater and greater sacrifices are being demanded of European taxpayers, at the same time as the frauds uncovered in 1996 amount to 1.4% of the budget."* And Anita Gradin, the commissioner in charge of fraud prevention, stated, *"Criminal organizations operate on the principle of minimum risk: they spread their different activities across the member States, choosing for each one that State where the risk is smallest."*

I poured Hélène Pessayre another glass of wine.

"It's delicious," she said.

I didn't know if she really meant it. Her thoughts seemed to be elsewhere. On Babette's disks. Or in the place where her father had met his death. Her eyes came to rest on me. Her look was tender and affectionate. I wanted to take her in my arms and hold her. Kiss her. But that was the last thing to do.

"We started receiving anonymous letters in the mail. I've never forgotten what the last one said. 'There's no point in trying to protect your family, or in scattering documents all over the country. Nothing escapes us. So please see reason and drop the case.'

"My mother refused to leave, and so did my brothers and I. We didn't really believe in these threats. 'They're just trying to intimidate us,' my father would say. Not that that stopped him from asking for police protection. The house was put under twenty-four-hour surveillance. And he had two inspectors with him everywhere he went. So did we, but more discreetly. I don't know how long we could have gone on living like that . . ." She broke off, and looked down at the wine in her glass. "One evening, he was found in the garage of our building. In his car, with his throat cut."

She looked up at me. The veil had gone from her eyes, and they had regained their dark brilliance.

"The weapon used was a double-edged knife, with a blade nearly six inches long and just one inch wide." It was the police captain speaking now. The crime expert. "The same one used on Sonia De Luca and Georges Mavros."

"You don't mean it's the same man?"

"No. The same weapon. The same type of knife. It struck me when I read the pathologist's report on Sonia. It took me back eight years, you know?"

I remembered what I'd thrown in her face on the terrace at Ange's, and suddenly I didn't feel proud of myself. "I'm sorry about what I said the other day."

She shrugged. "But it's true, I don't have anything else to do in my life. Only that. It was what I wanted. It was the only reason I became a cop. To fight crime. Especially organized crime. That's my life, now."

How could she be so determined? The words were cold, passionless, a statement of fact.

"You can't live for revenge," I said, imagining that was what drove her.

"Who said anything about revenge? I'm not out to avenge my father's death. All I'm trying to do is continue what he started. In my own way. In a different line of work. The killer was never arrested. In the end, the case was closed. That's why I made the choice I did. Why I joined the police." She drank some wine, then went on, "Revenge gets you nowhere. Neither does pessimism, like I said. You just have to be determined." She looked at me. "And realistic."

Realism. In my opinion, a word used to justify moral complacency, meanness, and the shameful sins of omission that men committed every day. Realism also allowed those who had power in this society—even just scraps, crumbs of power—to crush everyone else.

I preferred not to be drawn into an argument with her.

"Why aren't you saying anything?" she asked, with a touch of irony.

"Being a realist means getting screwed."

"My sentiments exactly." She smiled. "I only said it to see how you'd react."

"And I was afraid you were going to slap me."

She smiled again. I liked her smile. The dimples it made in her cheeks. I was becoming familiar with that smile. And with Hélène Pessayre.

"Fabio," she said.

It was the first time she'd called me by my first name. And I really liked the way she said it. I waited for the worst.

"I looked at the black disk. I read it."

"You're crazy!"

"It's really horrible."

It was as if she was paralyzed.

I held out my hand to her. She put her hand on mine and squeezed it. Hard. Everything that might or might not happen between us was contained in that touch.

First, I thought, we had to get out from under the stifling shadow of death. That was what her eyes also seemed to be saying at that moment. And it was like a cry. A silent cry at all the horrors still to come.

18.

IN WHICH THE LESS YOU CONCEDE TO
LIFE, THE CLOSER YOU GET TO DEATH

Those who are dead stay dead, I was thinking, still holding Hélène Pessayre's hand tightly in mine. But we have to carry on living.

"We have to beat death," I said.

She didn't seem to hear me. She was lost in thought, somewhere far away.

"Hélène," I said, applying a gentle pressure to her fingers.

"Yes, of course," she said. "Of course . . ."

She gave a weary smile, then slowly freed her hand from mine, stood up, and took a few steps around the room.

"It's a long time since I last had a man," she said in a low voice. "I mean, a man who didn't leave early the next morning, trying to find an excuse not to see me again that night, or any other night."

I stood up and walked toward her.

She was standing by the French window that led out onto my terrace. Her hands deep in the pockets of her jeans, like the other morning at the harbor. She was looking out into the darkness. Toward the open sea. Toward that other shore she had left once. I knew that if you'd been born in Algeria, if you'd grown up there, you could never forget it. Didier Perez never stopped talking about it. From having listened to him, I knew all the seasons of Algiers, its days and its nights. "The silences on summer evenings . . ." He always got a nostalgic look in his eyes when he said that. He missed the place desperately. Above all, those silences on summer evenings. Those brief moments he still thought of as a promise of happiness. I was sure Hélène felt the same thing in her heart.

She turned to look at me. "Absurdity reigns supreme, but love is the salvation, Camus said. All those corpses, the death I see around me every day . . . It's made love impossible for me. Even pleasure . . ."

"Hélène."

"Don't be embarrassed, Montale. It does me good to talk about these things. Especially with you."

I could feel her almost physically brooding on her past.

"The last man in my life . . ."

She took out the pack of cigarettes from the pocket of her shirt and offered me one. I lit hers for her.

"It's as if I was cold inside, you know? I loved him. But when he touched me, I . . . I didn't feel anything."

I'd never talked about these things with a woman. About what happens when the body closes up and doesn't respond.

For a long time, I'd tried to remember the last night Lole and I had made love. The last time we'd embraced as lovers. The last time she'd put her arm around my waist. I'd thought about it for hours, but I still couldn't remember. All I could remember was the night when I'd caressed her body for a long time and finally realized in despair that she was still completely dry.

"I don't want to," she'd said.

She'd snuggled against me and buried her head in the hollow of my shoulder. My cock had gone soft against her warm belly.

"It's not important," I'd murmured.

"Yes, it is."

She was right, it was important. We'd been making love less often for several months now, and every time Lole had felt less pleasure. On another occasion, as I was slowly moving back and forth inside her, I became aware that she was totally absent. Her body was there. But she was far away. Far already. I couldn't come. I slipped out of her. Neither of us moved. Neither of us said a word. We both drifted into sleep.

I looked at Hélène. "You just didn't love the man anymore. That's all."

"No . . . No, I loved him. I probably still love him. I don't know. I miss his hands on my body. It wakes me at night, sometimes. Though not so much now as it used to." She dragged pensively on her cigarette. "No, I think it's a lot more serious than that. I have the feeling that death is gradually casting a shadow over my life. And when you realize that's happening . . . how shall I put it . . . ? It's as if you're in the dark. You can't see anything anymore. Not even the face of the person you love. And all the people around you start thinking of you as being more dead than alive."

If I kissed her now, I told myself, it would be a hopeless gesture. I didn't consider it seriously. It was only a thought, a slightly crazy thought, an attempt not to be sucked in to the dizzying spiral of her words. The place she was going was a place I knew. I'd been there many times myself.

I was starting to understand what she was trying to say. It was all connected with Sonia's death. That death had reminded her of her father and, at the same time, of what her own life had become. Of all the things that unravel as you go on, as you make choices. And the less you concede to life, the closer you get to death. Thirty-four years old. The same age as Sonia. She'd said that several times, the other day, on the terrace at Ange's.

Sonia's sudden death, just when she had the possibility of a future with me, a future in love—maybe the only kind of future we still have left—had reminded Hélène of her own failures. Her own fears. I understood now why she'd been so insistent on knowing what I'd felt for Sonia that night.

"You know . . ." I began. But I left the sentence unfinished.

In my case, it was Mavros's death that had forever deprived me of my adolescence. My youth. Thanks to Mavros—even though we hadn't known each other well as children—I'd been able to bear first Manu's death, then Ugo's.

"What?" she asked.

"Nothing."

Now, my world was over. I had no idea what exactly that might mean, or what the consequences of it might be in the next few hours. I was starting to realize that now. I thought about what Hélène had just said. Like her, I was in the dark. I couldn't see anything. Only what lay immediately ahead. The things that needed to be done, and once done couldn't be undone. Like killing that Mafia son of a bitch.

She took a last drag on her cigarette, and put it out. Almost angrily. I looked her in the eyes, and she looked at me the same way.

"I think," she said, "that when something important is about to happen, we're somehow taken out of our normal state. Our thoughts, I mean, my thoughts, your thoughts, reach out to each other . . . Yours to mine, mine to yours . . . Do you understand what I'm saying?"

I didn't want to listen to her anymore. Not really. All I wanted was to hold her in my arms. I was only about three feet from her. I could put my hand on her shoulder, slide it down her back and take her by the waist. But I still wasn't sure it was what she wanted. What she expected of me. Not now. Two corpses lay between us, like a chasm separating us. All we could do was hold out our hands to each other. Taking care not to fall into the chasm.

"I think so," I said. "We can't live in each other's head. It's too scary. Is that what you mean?"

"More or less. Let's say it leaves us too exposed. If I . . . if we slept together, we'd be too vulnerable . . . afterwards."

"Afterwards" meant the hours to come. Babette's arrival. The confrontation with the Mafia guys. The choices to be made. Babette's and mine. Which weren't necessarily compatible. Hélène Pessayre's wish to control everything. And Honorine and Fonfon in the background. With their fear too.

"There's no rush," I replied, stupidly.

"You're talking crap. You want it as much as I do."

She'd turned to me, and I could see her chest rising slowly. Her lips were slightly parted, waiting only for my lips. I didn't move. Only our eyes dared meet.

"I felt it on the phone earlier. How much you wanted me. Am I right?"

I was incapable of saying a word.

"Say it."

"Yes, you're right."

"Please."

"Yes, I want you. I really want you."

Her eyes lit up.

Everything was possible.

I didn't move.

"So do I," she said, almost without moving her lips.

The woman could extract any words she wanted from me. If she'd asked me at that moment what time Babette was due in Marseilles, and where I was supposed to be meeting her, I'd have told her.

But she didn't ask me.

"So do I," she repeated. "I think I wanted it at the same moment. As if I'd been hoping you'd call just then . . . That's what I had in mind when I told you I was coming to see you. Sleeping with you. Spending the night in your arms."

"And did you change your mind on the way?"

"Yes," she said, with a smile. "I changed my mind, but the desire's still there."

Slowly, she held out her hand, and stroked my cheek with

her fingers. Very lightly. My cheek started to burn, much more so than after the slap.

"It's late," she said in a low voice. She smiled. A weary smile. "And I'm tired. But there's no rush, is there?"

"The awful thing," I said, trying to joke, "is that whatever I say to you, you always turn it against me."

"That's something you'll have to get used to with me."

She picked up her purse.

I couldn't keep her. We both had something to do. The same thing, or almost. But we wouldn't take the same path. She knew that, and I got the impression she'd finally admitted it. It wasn't just a question of trust anymore. Trust committed us too much to each other. We each had to go to our own limits. The limits of our solitude and our desires. At the end of it, we might find a truth. Death. Or life. Love. A relationship. Who could tell?

Superstitiously, I touched Didier Perez's ring with my thumb. And I remembered what he'd told me. "If it's written, it's written."

"I have something to tell you, Montale," she said, at the door. "It was the head of my squad who ordered your phone to be tapped. But I haven't been able to find out when."

"I assumed it was something like that. But what does it mean?"

"Just what you thought. In a while, I'm going to have to make a detailed report on those two murders. The motives behind them. The Mafia and all the rest of it . . . It's the pathologist who discovered the two murders were related. I'm not the only one to be interested in the Mafia's techniques. He passed on his findings to my superiors."

"And what about the disks?"

She was angry at me for asking the question. I could see it in her eyes.

"Hand them in with your report," I said, very quickly.

"There's no reasons to suppose your superior isn't straight, is there?"

"If I didn't hand them in," she replied, in a monotonous voice, "I'd be finished."

For a fraction of a second, we stood there looking at each other.

"Sleep well, Hélène."

"Thanks."

We couldn't shake hands. We couldn't kiss either. Hélène Pessayre left as she had come. Without the awkwardness.

"Call me, Montale," she said. "O.K.?"

Because it wasn't so easy to say goodbye. It was as though something was ending before it had even started.

I nodded, and watched her cross the street to her car. For a moment, I thought of how it might have been if we'd kissed. How gentle and tender the kiss would have been. Then I imagined the two Mafiosi and the two cops looking up drowsily as Hélène Pessayre passed, then going back to sleep, wondering if I'd fucked the captain or not. That was enough to drive any erotic thoughts from my head.

I poured myself a drop of Lagavulin and put on the album by Gianmaria Testa.

Un po' di là del mare c'è una terra sincera
Come gli occhi di tuo figlio quando ride

Words that stayed with me for the rest of the night. *Just beyond the sea, there's a land as genuine as the eyes of your son when he smiles.*

Sonia, I'll give your son his smile back. I'll do it for us, for what might have been between you and me, the love we might have shared, the life we might have had, the joy, the joys that linger beyond death, for the train going down to the sea, to Turchino, for the days yet to be created, the hours, the pleas-

ure, our bodies, our desires, and again our desires, and for
this song I'd have learned for you, this song I'd have sung, for
the simple pleasure of saying to you

Se vuoi restiamo insieme anche stasera

Saying it again and again, *If you like, we can stay together
this evening.*
Sonia.
I'll do it. For Enzo's smile.

By morning, the mistral had died down completely.
I listened to the news as I made my first coffee of the day.
The fire had gained more ground, but the tanker planes had
been able to go on the offensive at daybreak. There was
renewed hope that the fires could quickly be brought under
control.
My cup of coffee in one hand, a cigarette in the other, I
walked to the end of my terrace. The sea, calmer now, was
again a deep blue. This sea, I told myself, this sea that lapped
both Marseilles and Algiers, promised nothing, forecast nothing. All it did was give, but it gave in abundance. Maybe what
attracted Hélène and me to each other, I thought, wasn't love
after all. Just this shared feeling of being able to see things
clearly, which made us both inconsolable.
And tonight, I'd be seeing Babette.

19.

IN WHICH IT IS NECESSARY
TO KNOW HOW WE SEE THINGS

My heart skipped a beat. The shutters of Honorine's house were closed. We never closed our shutters in summer. We simply pulled them together, keeping the windows open, to benefit from a little cool air at night and in the early morning. I put down my cup and walked over to her terrace. The door was closed too. Locked. Even when she "went into town," Honorine never took so many precautions.

I quickly pulled on a pair of jeans and a T-shirt, didn't bother to comb my hair, and ran to Fonfon's. He was behind the bar counter, absently leafing through *La Marseillaise*.

"Where is she?" I asked.

"Can I make you a coffee?"

"Fonfon!"

"Fuck it!" he said, putting a saucer in front of me. His eyes were redder than usual, and full of sadness. "I took her away."

"What?"

"This morning. Alex drove us. I have a cousin in Les Caillols. That's where I took her. She'll be fine there . . . I thought maybe a few days . . ."

He'd had the same idea I'd had for Mavros, then for Bruno and his family. All at once, I felt angry at myself for not suggesting it to Honorine, or to Fonfon. After the conversation he and I had had, it should have been obvious. The fear that something might happen to Honorine. Fonfon had managed to convince her. She'd agreed to go. They'd decided it between them, and hadn't said a word about it to me. Because it was none of my business now, it was their business, just the two of them. Hélène Pessayre's slap in the face was nothing compared to this.

"You could have said something," I said harshly. "You could have come and woken me up, given me a chance to say goodbye!"

"That's how it is, Fabio. No need to get upset. I did what I thought was best."

"I'm not upset."

No, upset wasn't the word. But I couldn't find the right words. My life was going to hell, and even Fonfon didn't trust me anymore. That's what it came down to.

"Didn't it occur to you those scumbags outside could have followed you?"

"Of course it occurred to me!" he cried, putting the cup of coffee on the saucer. "What do you think I am? Stupid or something? Senile?"

"Give me a cognac."

Nervously, he got the bottle and a glass, and served me. We didn't take our eyes off each other.

"Fifi had to keep an eye on the road. If any car we didn't know had started after us, he'd have called Alex on his cellphone in the taxi, and we'd have come back."

The old bastard! I thought.

I knocked the cognac back in one go. I immediately felt the warmth of it spread to the pit of my stomach. Sweat broke out all over my back. "And you're sure no one followed you?"

"The guys in the Fiat Punto weren't there this morning. Just the cops. And they didn't move."

"How can you be sure they were cops?"

"You just have to look at them to know that."

I drank some of the coffee. "And you say the Fiat Punto wasn't there?"

"It still isn't."

What was going on? Two days, the killer had said. I couldn't believe he'd swallowed everything I'd told him. I knew he thought of me as just a poor shmuck, but even so!

I had a sudden vision of horror. The killers driving up to Le Castellas to corner Babette. I shook my head, dismissing the idea. Convincing myself that my phone had only been tapped since last night, that the links between the cops and the Mafia weren't as strong as all that. No, I thought, trying to put my mind at rest, it couldn't have been the head of Hélène's squad. But it could have been one of his men. Any one of them. It only took one. One who took the plunge. Just one, Goddammit!

"Can you pass me the phone?"

"Here you go," Fonfon said, putting it on the counter. "You want to eat something?"

I shrugged, and dialed the number of Le Castellas. At the other end, the phone rang six, seven, eight times. The sweat was pouring off me. Nine times.

At last someone answered, in an authoritative-sounding voice. "Lieutenant Brémond."

My body went hot and cold, and my legs started shaking. They'd been there. They knew about my phone calls. I started shaking from head to foot.

"Hello?"

Slowly, I put down the receiver.

"Grilled *fegatelli*, that O.K.?" Fonfon called from the kitchen.

"Fine."

I dialed Hélène Pessayre's number.

"Hélène," I said, when she answered.

"Is everything O.K.?"

"No. It's not O.K. I think they've been up to Le Castellas, where Babette was staying. I think something's happened. No, I don't think it, I'm sure of it! I called, and a cop answered. Lieutenant Brémond."

"Where is that?"

"The Saint-Jean-du-Gard district."

"I'll call you back." But she didn't hang up. "Was Babette up there?"

"No, in Nîmes. She's in Nîmes."

It was a lie. Babette must have taken the train by now. At least, I hoped so.

"Oh," was all Hélène Pessayre said.

She hung up.

The smell of *fegatelli* was starting to spread through the bar. I wasn't hungry, but it smelled great. I had to eat. Drink less. Eat. Smoke less.

Eat.

"You'll have some, won't you?" Fonfon asked, coming out of the kitchen.

He put plates, glasses, knives and forks on a table facing the sea. Then he opened a bottle of Saint-Cannat rosé, a nice little wine from a cooperative, ideal for morning snacks.

"Why didn't you stay with her?"

He went back into the kitchen. I heard him turning the *fegatelli* over on the grill. I went in to him.

"Why, Fonfon?"

"What?"

"Why didn't you stay with your cousin too?"

He looked at me, and I couldn't tell what was in his eyes. "I'll tell you . . ." I saw his anger rising. "Where would Félix have called you, huh?" he exploded. "To tell you when he was taking Babette out in his boat? You asked him to call here, in my bar."

"He was the one who suggested it and—"

"Right. So I guess he's not stupid or senile either."

"Is that all you stayed for? I could have—"

"Could have what? Hung around here, waiting for the phone to ring? Like now." He turned the *fegatelli* over again. "Nearly ready." He slid all of it onto a dish, took some bread, and went out to the table.

I followed him. "Did Félix call you?"

"No, I called him. Yesterday. Before our little conversation. I wanted to know something."

"What did you want to know?"

"How serious this thing really is. So I asked him if you'd been to see him to get . . . you know, to get Manu's gun. He told me you had. He told me everything."

"You already knew everything last night?"

"Yeah."

"And you didn't say anything."

"I needed to hear it from you. I needed to hear you tell me. Me, Fonfon!"

"Fuck it!"

"And you know something, Fabio? I don't think you told us everything. Neither does Félix. But he doesn't give a damn. He told me. He may pretend, but he doesn't care much about life anymore. You see . . . No, you don't see. Sometimes you don't see anything. You just pass by . . ."

Fonfon lowered his head over the plate and started eating. I couldn't eat. After three mouthfuls, and a lot of silence, he looked up. His eyes were misty with tears. "Eat, dammit! It'll get cold."

"Fonfon . . ."

"Let me tell you this. I'm here to . . . to be with you. But I don't know why, Fabio. I really don't know why! It was Honorine who asked me to stay. She wouldn't have gone otherwise. That was her one condition. Do you hear what I'm saying?" He stood up abruptly, put his hands flat on the table, and leaned toward me. "Because if she hadn't asked me, I don't know if I'd have stayed."

He went to the kitchen. I stood up and went to join him. He was standing with his head against the freezer, crying. I put my arms around his shoulders. "Fonfon," I said.

He turned slowly, and I hugged him. He was still crying, like a little boy.

What a mess, Babette. What a mess.

But Babette wasn't responsible for all this. She was just the catalyst. And I was discovering my true nature. Someone who didn't pay any attention even to those he loved. Someone who didn't listen to their anxieties, their fears. Their desire to live, and be happy, a little while longer. I was living in a world that had no room for them. I rubbed shoulders with them, but I didn't share. I took everything they gave me, without really caring, and if ever they said or did anything I didn't like, I'd let it go, out of pure laziness.

When you came down to it, that was why Lole had left me. Because of the way I passed people by, apathetic, unconcerned. Uninterested. Even at the worst times, I didn't know how to show them how fond of them I really was. I didn't know how to say it either. I thought things like friendship and love were obvious. Hélène Pessayre was right. I hadn't given everything to Lole. I'd never given everything to anyone.

I'd lost Lole. And now I was losing Fonfon and Honorine. And that was the worst thing that could happen. Because without them, I'd be without my last bearings. They were beacons at sea, lighting me the way to harbor. Showing me my route.

"I love you, both of you. I love you, Fonfon."

He lifted his eyes to me, then freed himself. "All right, all right," he said.

"You're all I have left, dammit!"

"Oh, yes!" His anger exploded again. "Now you remember! Now that we're almost like family! But the killers are out there, prowling . . . And the cops are tapping your phone without telling that captain of yours . . . You're worried, of course, you even go to get a gun. But what about us? Are you worried about us? Oh, no! We just have to wait until Monsieur sorts it all out. Until everything goes back to normal. And afterwards, if we're still alive, we'll go back to our old routine. Fishing, aperitifs, *pétanque*, rummy in the evening . . . Is that it, Fabio? Is that how you see things? Who are we to you, huh? Tell us that!"

"No," I said in a low voice. "That's not how I see things."

"O.K., so how do you see them, huh?"

The phone rang.

"Montale?"

Hélène Pessayre's voice was flat. Toneless.

"Yup."

"Around seven o'clock this morning, Bruno went crazy . . ."

I closed my eyes. The images came charging into my head. Not even images, just rivers of blood.

"He killed his wife and his two children. With . . . with an axe. It's . . ."

She couldn't say anything more.

"What about him, Hélène?"

"He hanged himself. Simple as that."

Fonfon came up to me quietly, and placed a glass of rosé in front of me. I drank it in one go, and made a sign for him to pour me another. He put the bottle next to me.

"What do the cops say?"

"They're classing it as a domestic."

I drank another glass of rosé. "Of course."

"According to witnesses, things hadn't been going too well between Bruno and his wife for some time . . . Apparently, there'd been a lot of talk in the village about this woman who was living in their house."

"That'd surprise me. No one knew Babette was in Le Castellas."

"There are witnesses, Montale. At least one. An old friend of Bruno's. The park ranger."

"Of course," I repeated.

"They've issued your friend's description. They'd like to talk to her."

"What does that mean?"

"It means she has the cops on her trail, and behind them the Mafia guys. The killer, just waiting to trap her."

If Bruno had talked—and there was no way he hadn't—the Mafiosi must have charged down to Nîmes, where Babette was supposed to be spending the night with friends. I hoped she'd left before they got there. For her sake. And the sake of her hosts. I hoped she was already on the train.

"Montale, where is she?"

"I don't know. I really don't. She might be on a train. She was due to be coming to Marseilles today. She's supposed to be phoning me when she arrives."

"Did you have anything planned for when she arrives?"

"Yes."

"And was calling me part of your plan?"

"Not straight away. Later."

I heard her breathing.

"I'm sending a team to the station. In case those scumbags are there and try something."

"I'd prefer it if she wasn't followed."

"Are you afraid I'll find out where she's going?"

My turn to take a deep breath. "Yes," I said. "It'll endanger someone else. And you aren't sure of anything. Or anybody. Not even your closest colleague, Béraud, am I right?"

"I know where she's going, Montale. I think I know where you're going to meet her tonight."

I poured myself another glass of wine. I felt unsteady on my feet. "Did you have me followed?"

"No. I was ahead of you. You told me the person you were supposed to see, Félix, lived in Vallon-des-Auffes. I sent Béraud. He was walking around the harbor when you got there."

"You didn't trust me, huh?"

"I still don't. But it's better this way. For now. Each of us playing our own game. That's what you wanted, isn't it?"

I heard her breathing again, as if she was suffocating.

When she spoke again, her voice was lower, huskier. "I still hope we can see each other when all this is over."

"I hope so too, Hélène."

"I've never been as sincere with a man as I was with you last night."

She hung up.

Fonfon was sitting at the table. He hadn't finished his *fegatelli*, and I hadn't even started mine. He watched me as I walked toward him. He looked exhausted.

"Fonfon, go join Honorine. Tell her I'm the one who decides. Not her. Tell her I want you to be together. There's nothing for you to do here!"

"How about you?"

"I'm going to wait for Félix to call me, and then I'll close the bar. Leave me a number where I can reach you."

He stood up, and looked me straight in the eyes. "What are you going to do?"

"I'm going to kill a man, Fonfon. I'm going to kill a man."

20.

IN WHICH THERE IS NO TRUTH THAT DOESN'T CARRY WITHIN IT ITS OWN BITTERNESS

Now that the mistral had died down, the smell of burning hung in the air. An acrid mixture of wood, resin, and chemicals. The firefighters seemed finally to have gotten the fire under control. The talk now was of eight thousand, five hundred and twenty acres destroyed. Mainly forest. Someone on the radio, I couldn't remember who, had mentioned the figure of a million trees burned. Which made this fire comparable to the one in 1989.

After a short nap, I'd set off for a walk in the *calanques*. I needed to cleanse my mind with the beauty of the landscape. To empty it of nasty thoughts, and fill it with sublime images. I also needed to fill my poor lungs with some clean air.

I'd started out from the harbor of Calelongue, close by Les Goudes. An easy walk, only two hours, along the customs path. With magnificent views of the Riou archipelago and the southern slopes of the *calanques*. When I got to the Plan des Cailles, I turned off the path into the woods above the *calanque* of Les Queyrons, staying close to the sea. I'd come to a halt, sweating and panting, at the end of the coastal path overlooking the *calanque* of Podestat.

It felt good to be up here, facing the sea. In the silence. There was nothing to understand here, nothing to know. Everything was just there to be seen and enjoyed.

Just before I left, Félix had phoned. It was a little before two o'clock. Babette had just arrived. He put her on. She hadn't taken the train at Nîmes after all. When she got to the station, she told me, she'd had a kind of premonition. She'd gone into a car rental office, and had come out at the wheel of a Peugeot 205. Once in Marseilles, she'd parked her car in the harbor area and taken a bus up onto the Corniche. Then she'd walked down to Vallon-des-Auffes.

I'd closed the bar, pulled the shutters over the windows that looked out to sea, and let down the metal shutter. The room was only dimly lit now by a skylight above the front door.

"I needed that," she began. "To let the city enter me. To be filled with its light. I even stopped at La Samaritaine for a drink and a bite to eat. I was thinking of you. Of what you often say. That you can't understand anything about this city if you're indifferent to its light."

"Babette . . ."

"I love this city. I watched the people around me. On the terrace. On the street. Envying them. They were alive. Their lives may be good or bad, they may have their ups and downs, like everyone. But they were alive . . . I felt like someone from another planet."

"Babette . . ."

"Wait . . . I took off my sunglasses and closed my eyes and felt the sun on my face, the way you do when you're on the beach. I was starting to be myself again. I told myself, 'You're home.' But, you know what, Fabio?"

"What?"

"It isn't true. I'm not really at home here anymore. I can't walk down the street without wondering if I'm being followed."

She'd fallen silent for a moment. I'd pulled on the phone wire and sat down on the floor, with my back against the counter. I was tired. I was sleepy. I needed air. The one thing I didn't want was to hear what she was going to say, which I could sense coming with every word she spoke.

"I've been thinking," Babette said. Her voice was strangely calm, which made it all the more unbearable. "I'll never feel at home again in Marseilles if I give up on the investigation. I've spent years working on it. I have to see it through. People here are like that, they always have to see things through, even if they sometimes take them to extremes. Even if it proves their undoing . . ."

"Babette, I don't want to discuss this over the phone."

"I wanted you to know, Fabio. Last night, I'd come to the conclusion that you were right. I'd weighed it all up. But . . . coming here . . . the pleasure of feeling the sun on my skin, the light in my eyes . . . I know I'm right."

"Do you have the papers with you?" I cut in. "The originals?"

"No. They're in a safe place."

"Dammit, Babette!" I cried.

"There's no point in getting worked up about it, that's how it is. How can we live happily if every time we go somewhere or buy something, we know we're being fucked by the Mafia? Huh? Really fucked!"

Whole sections of her report passed in front of my eyes. As if, that night at Cyril's, I'd inserted the computer's hard disk in my head.

It is in the tax havens that the crime syndicates make contact with the world's great commercial banks through their local subsidiaries, which specialize in offering a discreet, personalized service to those with high-yield accounts. The opportunities for tax evasion are seized upon by both legitimate businesses and criminal organizations. New developments in banking techniques and telecommunications in fact offer many opportunities for the rapid circulation and disappearance of profits from illegal transactions.

"Fabio?"

I blinked.

The money can easily be moved by electronic transfer from the parent company to a subsidiary registered as a dummy company in a tax haven. Billions of dollars coming from banks man-

aging institutional funds—including pension funds, savings banks and treasury funds—circulate in this way, moving into accounts registered in Luxemburg, the Channel Islands, the Cayman Islands, and so on.

As a consequence of tax evasion, the accumulation in tax havens of enormous capital reserves belonging to large companies is also responsible for the increase in the budget deficit of most Western countries . . .

"That's not the question," I said.

"Oh, really? Then what is?"

She hadn't talked about Bruno. I assumed she didn't know anything about the massacre. I decided I wouldn't say anything. Not for the moment. I'd keep that atrocity as my trump card. When we finally met. Tonight.

"It's not a question. I know I'll never be happy again if . . . if those scumbags do what they did to Sonia and Mavros, and cut Honorine's and Fonfon's throats!"

"I've seen blood, too!" she said losing her temper. "I saw Gianni's body. His mutilated body. So, don't talk to me about—"

"But you're alive, dammit! They aren't! And I'm alive! And Honorine, and Fonfon, and Félix, too, for the moment! I don't give a fuck what you've seen! Because at the rate you're going, you're going to see a lot more. And a lot worse! Your own body being cut up piece by piece . . ."

"Stop!"

"Until you tell them where those fucking papers are. I'm sure you'll crack as soon as they cut off the first finger."

"You bastard!" she screamed.

I wondered where Félix was. Was he drinking a glass of cold beer, reading an issue of *Les Pieds Nickelés*, and ignoring what he was hearing? Or had he gone out to the harbor so Babette could talk without feeling she was being spied on?

"Where's Félix?"

"In the harbor. Getting the boat ready. He said he'd put to sea around eight."

"Good."

Silence again.

The semi-darkness in the bar was doing me good. I felt like lying down on the floor and going to sleep. For a long time. Hoping that while I slept this whole huge mess would disappear and I'd dream of the dawn coming up pure and clear over the sea.

"Fabio," Babette said.

I remembered thinking, at the top of the Cortiou pass, that there's no truth that doesn't carry within it its own bitterness. I'd read that somewhere.

"Babette, I don't want anything to happen to you. I couldn't live either if . . . if he killed you. All the people I loved are dead. My friends. And Lole left . . ."

"Oh!"

I'd never answered Babette's letter, the letter Lole had opened and read. The letter that had split us up. I'd been angry at Lole for prying into my secrets. Then at Babette. But neither Babette nor Lole were responsible for what had followed. The letter had arrived just when Lole was having severe doubts about me, and about her. About us, our life together.

"You know, Fabio," she'd said to me one night, one of those nights when I was still trying to convince her to wait, to stay. "My mind is made up. It's been made up a long time. I've given myself plenty of time to think. This has nothing to do with that letter from your friend Babette. That just helped me come to a decision . . . I've had my doubts for a long time. This isn't a sudden whim. Which makes it even worse, in a way. I know . . . I know I just have to leave."

The only thing I could find to say in reply was that she was stubborn. And too proud to admit she was wrong. Too proud to make a U-turn and come back to me. To us.

"Stubborn? You're as stubborn as I am! No . . ."

What she said next finally closed the door on our relationship.

"To live with a man I need to love him, and I don't feel that love for you anymore."

Later, on another occasion, Lole had asked me if I'd answered that girl, Babette.

"No," I'd said.

"Why?"

Because I couldn't find the words to write back, or even to call her. What could I say to Babette? That I hadn't known how fragile my relationship with Lole was. That I supposed all genuine relationships were like that. As brittle as glass. That love pushes people to the limit. And that what she, Babette, thought was love was only an illusion.

I hadn't found the courage to say those things. Or even to say that, although the prospect of Lole's going had left me feeling empty inside, I didn't see any point in our getting together again.

"Because I don't love her, you must know that," I'd replied to Lole.

"You might be wrong."

"Lole, please."

"You spend your whole life not wanting to admit things. You don't want to admit I'm leaving, and you don't want to admit she's waiting for you."

For the first time, I'd wanted to slap her.

"I didn't know," Babette said.

"Forget it. The important thing is what's happening now. These killers on our trail. That's what we have to talk about tonight. I have a few ideas. For how we can negotiate with them."

"We'll see, Fabio . . . But you know . . . I think the only

solution is to have some kind of 'clean hands' operation in France. It's the only way, the only most effective way, to answer people's skepticism. No one believes in anything anymore. Not in politicians. Not in the political process. Not in the values of this country. It's . . . it's the only way to counter the National Front. Bring it all out in the open. Wash our dirty linen in public."

"You must be dreaming! What did it change in Italy?"

"It changed some things."

"Oh, sure."

She was right, of course. And there were quite a few judges in France who thought the same. They kept going, courageously, case by case. Often working alone. Sometimes risking their lives. Like Hélène Pessayre's father. I knew all that, of course.

But I also knew that simply making a fuss in the media wouldn't give this country back its morality. I didn't believe journalists were really interested in the truth. The TV news was just a distraction. All those images of genocide, first in Bosnia, then in Rwanda, now in Algeria, hadn't brought millions of citizens out on the streets, in France or anywhere else. They read about earthquakes, or railroad disasters, and turned over the page. Leaving the truth to those it concerned. And those it concerned were the poor, not people who were happy or thought they were.

"You said it yourself," I said. "The fight against the Mafia can only succeed if there's simultaneous progress in economic and social development."

"That doesn't mean we shouldn't tell the truth when the moment is right. And this is the moment, Fabio."

"Bullshit!"

"Fuck you, Fabio! Do you want me to hang up?"

"How many deaths is the truth worth?"

"You can't think like that. That's the way losers think."

"We are losers!" I screamed. "We won't change anything. Not anymore."

I thought again about what Hélène Pessayre had said, when we were at the Fort Saint-Jean. About that book on the World Bank. About this enclosed world that was shaping up, and how we'd be excluded from it. How we were already excluded. On one side, the civilized West, on the other the "dangerous classes" of the South, the Third World. And the frontier between them. The *limes*.

A new world.

I knew I had no place in it.

"I refuse to listen to this bullshit."

"All right, then, Babette, go ahead, dammit! Publish your report and die, let's all die, you, me, Honorine, Fonfon, Félix . . ."

"You want me to go away, is that it?"

"Where do you think you can go, you stupid bitch?" And the words slipped out. "This morning, the Mafia took an axe to your friend Bruno and his family . . ."

Silence. A silence as heavy as the four coffins that would soon be lowered into the ground.

"I'm sorry, Babette. They thought you were up there."

She was crying. I could hear her. Big tears, I imagined. Not sobs, just tears. Tears of panic and fear.

"I want it to end," she said softly.

"It'll never end, Babette. Because it's already ended. You just don't want to admit it. But we can get out of it. We can survive. For a while, a few years. Love each other. Believe in life. In beauty . . . And even put our trust in the law and the police of this country."

"You're a fool," she said.

And then the sobs started.

21.

IN WHICH IT BECOMES OBVIOUS
THAT ROTTENNESS IS BLIND

I sailed my boat into the harbor of the Frioul. It was exactly nine o'clock. The sea was rougher than I'd thought when I left Les Goudes. Babette must have been feeling pretty uncomfortable for the last thirty minutes, I thought, as I reduced speed. But I was bringing something to cheer her up. Sausage from Arles, wild boar pâté, six small goat's cheeses from Banon, and two bottles of Bandol red, from the Cagueloup estate. And my bottle of Lagavulin, for later in the evening. Before putting to sea again. I knew Félix wouldn't turn up his nose at that.

I was tense. For the first time, I'd set out to sea with an aim, a specific purpose. And that had started my head spinning with thoughts and questions. At one point, I'd even wondered how I could have reached my age and still had only a vague idea of what I was and what I wanted in life. I didn't know the answer to that one. There'd been other questions, more specific ones, that I'd tried to dismiss. The last was the simplest. What the hell was I doing here tonight, on my boat, with a gun, a 6.35, in my jacket pocket?

Because, after some hesitation, I'd brought Manu's gun with me. Ever since Honorine and Fonfon had left, I'd been feeling helpless. I'd lost my bearings. I was alone. At one point, I'd almost phoned Lole. To hear her voice. But what would I have said to her? The place where she was now was nothing like here. People weren't being murdered there. Instead, they loved each other. She and her friend, at least.

I'd started to feel very afraid.

As I'd gotten my boat out, I'd asked myself: What if you're

wrong, Fabio, and they sense you're up to something and follow you out to sea? I'd just come back from buying a few packs of cigarettes, during which I'd noticed that the Fiat Punto wasn't parked anywhere in the vicinity. I'd walked up the road to the end of the village. There wasn't any white Peugeot 304 either. No killers, no cops. That was when I'd felt my stomach tighten with fear. It was like an alarm bell ringing. This wasn't normal, they should have been there. The killers, because they hadn't yet laid their hands on Babette. The cops, because Hélène Pessayre had said she'd see to it. But it was too late. By now, Félix was already at sea.

I spotted Félix's boat, over to the right of the sea wall linking the islands of Pomègues and Ratonneau. On the built-up side, where there were a few bars open. The harbor was quiet. Even in summer, the Frioul didn't attract crowds in the evening. People from Marseilles only came here during the day. Over the years, there'd been lots of construction projects that had come to nothing. The Frioul islands weren't a place to live, just a place where people came to dive, fish and swim in the cold waters of the open sea.

"Félix!" I called, moving my boat closer to his.

He didn't move. He seemed to be asleep. Bent forward slightly.

The hull of my boat rubbed gently against his.

"Félix."

I put out my hand to give him a gentle shake. His head lolled to the side, then back, and his dead eyes looked into mine. From his open neck, the blood still gushed.

They were here.

Babette, I thought.

We were cornered. And Félix was dead.

Where was Babette?

There was a sudden groundswell, which made my stomach

heave, and the acid taste of bile was in my throat. I bent double. To vomit. But there was nothing in my stomach, just the Lagavulin I'd drunk when I was halfway here.

Félix.

His dead eyes. Dead forever.

And the blood was gushing. It would gush in my memory for the rest of my fucking life.

Félix.

I couldn't stay here.

I quickly leaned on his hull, pushed my boat away, started the motor, and reversed until I was free. I looked around at the harbor, the sea wall, the surrounding area. Nobody. I heard laughter coming from a sailboat. A man and a woman. The woman's laughter sparkled like champagne. They'd be making love soon. Lying naked on the deck, in the moonlight.

I took my boat far out to the east side of the island, which wasn't lit. I peered into the darkness. The white rock. Then I saw them. There were three of them. Bruscati and the driver. And the son of a bitch with the knife. They were quickly climbing the narrow path that leads up through the rocky ground to a multitude of small creeks.

They must be following Babette.

"Montale!"

I froze. The voice was familiar. A figure emerged from the shadow of a rock. It was Béraud, Alain Béraud, from Hélène Pessayre's team.

"I saw you arrive," he said, jumping nimbly into my boat. "But I don't think they did."

"What the hell are you doing here? Is she here too?"

"No."

I saw the three men disappear over the brow of the hill.

"How did those bastards find out?"

"I don't know."

"What do you mean, you don't know, for fuck's sake?" I

cried. I felt like shaking him. Strangling him. "So what are you doing here?"

"I was at Vallon-des-Auffes earlier."

"Why?"

"Fuck it, Montale! Didn't she tell you? We knew your girl friend was going to see that guy. I was there when you went to see him the other day."

"Yes, I know."

"Hélène figured it out. That you'd use the boat . . . Clever."

"Don't fuck me around, dammit!"

"She didn't like the idea of you being here without protection."

"But they whacked Félix. Where were you when that happened?"

"On my way. In fact, I only just got here." For a brief moment, he paused for thought. "I was the last to leave. That's the stupid part. I should have come here directly. And waited. But I . . . We weren't sure this was where you were meeting. It could have been the Château d'If. Or Planier . . . It could have been anywhere . . ."

"Right."

I didn't understand any of it anymore, but it didn't matter. We had to hurry up and find Babette. She had one advantage over the killers: she knew the island like the back of her hand. Every creek. Every rocky path. She'd been coming here for years, to dive.

"We'd better get going," I said. I thought for a moment. "I'll sail along the coast. Try to pick her up from one of the creeks. I can't see any other way."

"I'll go on foot," he said. "Along the path. Keeping behind them. O.K.?"

"O.K."

I started the motor. "Béraud," I said.

"Yeah?"

"Why are you on your own?"

"It's my day off," he replied. He wasn't joking.

"What do you mean?" I cried.

"That's the thing, Montale. We've been booted out. They took her off the case after she handed in her report."

We looked at each other, and in his eyes I thought I saw some of Hélène's rage and disgust.

"They really hauled her over the coals."

"Who's taken over the case?"

"It's with the Fraud Squad. But I don't know who's in charge yet."

I was overcome with anger. "Don't tell me she told them about your stakeout!"

"No."

I grabbed him by his shirt collar. "So how come they're here? Don't you know?"

"Yes . . . I think I do." His voice was calm.

"Who was it?"

"The driver. Our driver. It had to be him."

"Shit!" I said, letting him go. "And where's Hélène now?"

"At Septèmes-les-Vallons. Investigating the possibility the fires were started deliberately . . . Apparently, all hell's broken loose . . . She asked me not to let you out of my sight." He jumped out of the boat. "Montale," he said.

"What?"

"I bound and gagged the guy who was driving their speed-boat. And I called the cops. They should be here soon."

As he set off along the path, he took out his gun. It was a big one. I took out mine. Manu's gun. I inserted a cartridge clip and put on the safety.

I sailed slowly around the outside of the island, trying to spot either Babette or the killers. The white moonlight made the rocky ground look like a lunar landscape. These islands had never looked so grim.

I thought again about what Hélène Pessayre had said this morning on the phone. "Each of us playing our own game." She'd played hers and lost. I was playing mine, and I was losing too. "That's what you wanted, isn't it?" Had I screwed up again? Would we even be here if . . .

I saw Babette. She was climbing down a narrow, rocky gully.

I took the boat in closer. Keeping to the middle of the creek.

Call her, now. No, not yet. Let her come down. Let her get to the bottom of the creek.

I moved in a little closer, then cut the motor and glided slowly over the water, which was still quite deep. I picked up the oars and moved even closer.

Babette appeared on the narrow sandbank.

"Babette!" I called.

But she didn't hear me. She was looking up at the rocks. I thought I could hear her panting in fear. Panic. But it wasn't her, it was only my heart, pounding. Like a time bomb. Calm down, dammit! I told myself. You're going to explode!

Calm down! Calm down.

"Babette!" I cried.

She turned and saw me at last. And understood. At the same moment, the guy appeared. What he was holding wasn't just a pistol.

"Hide!" I yelled.

There was a volley of shots, covering my voice. Then more volleys. Babette got up, as if about to dive, then fell again. Into the water. The shooting stopped abruptly and I saw the killer turn and run. His submachine gun tumbled down onto the loose stones. Then, suddenly, there was silence. A moment later, his body crashed onto the rocks below. The impact of his skull on the rocks echoed through the creek.

Beraud's aim had been good.

I rowed like crazy until I felt the hull hit the rocks. I jumped out of the boat. Babette's body was still in the water. Motionless. I tried to lift it. It felt like lead.

"Babette," I wept. "Babette."

I gently pulled Babette's body toward the sand. There were eight bullet holes in her back. Slowly, I turned her over.

Babette. I lay down beside her.

The face I'd loved. Looking the same as ever. As beautiful as ever. The way Botticelli had dreamed it one night. The way he'd painted it the next day. The birthday of the world. Venus. Babette. Slowly, I stroked her forehead, then her cheek. I touched her lips with my fingers. Lips that had kissed me. That had covered my body with kisses. Sucked my cock. Her lips.

Like a madman, I covered her mouth with mine.

Babette.

The taste of salt. I thrust my tongue into her mouth, as far as it would go. In an impossible kiss, a kiss I wanted her to carry away with her. My tears ran. They were salty, too. They ran onto her open eyes. I kissed death. Passionately. Looking into her eyes. That was love. Looking into one another's eyes. And this was death. Not taking our eyes off one another.

Babette.

Her body moved convulsively. I had the taste of blood in my mouth. And I vomited the one thing I still had left to vomit. Life.

"Hello, asshole."

The voice. The voice I'd have recognized anywhere.

Shots echoed above us.

I didn't stand. I turned slowly, still sitting with my ass in the wet sand and my hands in the pockets of my jacket. With my right hand, I lifted the safety on my gun. After that, I didn't move.

He was aiming a gun in my direction, a big Colt. He looked me up and down. I couldn't see his eyes. Rottenness has no eyes, I thought. It's blind. I imagined his eyes when he looked at a woman's body. When he fucked her. Could you be fucked by Evil?

Yes. I had been.

"You tried to fuck us over, huh?"

I felt the contempt in his voice. As if he'd spat in my face.

"There's no point to this anymore," I said. "Killing her, or me. Tomorrow morning, the whole thing will be on the Internet. The complete list."

I'd called Cyril before I left. I'd told him to put it all out there, tonight. Without waiting to see what Babette thought.

He laughed. "The Internet?"

"Everyone will be able to read those fucking lists."

"Shut up, asshole. Where are the originals?"

I shrugged. "She didn't have time to tell me, dickhead. That's what we came here for."

More shots, up there on the rocks. Béraud was alive. At least for the moment.

"Right," the hitman said. He moved forward. He was a few feet from me now. His gun pointing right at me.

"Where's your knife?" I said. "Did you break it on my old friend?"

He laughed again. "Would you have preferred it if I cut you up too, asshole?"

Now, I told myself.

My finger on the trigger.

Shoot!

"Would you let me kill him? All of you?"

Shoot, dammit! Mavros screamed. Sonia started screaming too. And Félix. And Babette. Shoot! they were yelling. Fonfon, with anger in his eyes. Honorine, looking at me sadly. "The most honorable thing a survivor can do . . ." Shoot!

Fuck it, Montale, kill him! Kill him!

"I'm going to kill him."

Shoot!

Slowly he took aim at my head.

Shoot!

"Enzo!" I cried.

I fired. I emptied the whole cartridge into him.

He collapsed. The nameless killer. The voice. The voice of death. Death itself.

I started shaking. My hand still tight on the grip of the gun. Move, Montale. Move, don't stay here. I got up. I was shaking more and more.

"Montale!" Béraud called.

He wasn't far now. Another shot. Then silence.

Béraud didn't call again.

I walked unsteadily toward the boat. I looked at the gun in my hand. Manu's gun. With a violent movement, I flung it away from me, out to sea. It fell in the water, making almost the same noise—in my head it was the same noise—as the bullet that entered my back. I felt the bullet, but I didn't hear the shot until afterwards. Though it must have been the other way around.

I took a few steps in the water. With my hand, I stroked the open wound. The blood felt hot on my fingers. There was a burning sensation inside me. It was gaining ground, like the fire in the hills. The acres of my life were going up in smoke.

Sonia, Mavros, Félix, Babette. We'd all been consumed in the fire. The evil was spreading, engulfing the planet. It was too late. Hell had arrived.

Yes, but you're O.K., aren't you, Fabio? You're O.K., right? Right. It's only a bullet. Did it come out the other side? No, dammit. I don't think so.

I collapsed into the boat. Headlong. The motor. Start the

motor. I started the motor. Go home now. I was going home. It's over, Fabio.

I picked up the bottle of Lagavulin, opened it, and lifted it to lips. I felt the liquid going down. It was warm. It felt good. You couldn't grasp life, you just had to live it. What? Nothing. I was tired. Very tired. Sleep, yes. But don't forget to invite Hélène to lunch. On Sunday. Yes, Sunday. When's Sunday? Dammit, Fabio, don't fall asleep. The boat. You need to steer the boat. Go home. To Les Goudes.

The boat was heading out to sea. Everything was fine now. The whisky was trickling over my chin and down my neck. I couldn't feel anything anymore. In my body or in my head. The pain was gone. All my pains. All my fears. Fear itself.

Now I am death

I'd read that somewhere . . . Try to remember.
I am death.
Lole, could you draw the curtains on our life? Please. I'm tired.
Please, Lole.

The analysis of the Mafia presented in this novel derives in large part from official documents, in particular *United Nations World Summit for Social Development: The Globalization of Crime* (United Nations Public Information Department), as well as two articles that appeared in *Le Monde Diplomatique*: "Europe's Confetti Money in the Great Planetary Casino," by Jean Chesneaux (January 1996) and "How Organized Crime Is Poisoning the World Economy" by Michel Chossudovsky (December 1996). Many of the facts mentioned have also been reported in *Le Canard Enchaîné*, *Le Monde* and *Libération*.

ABOUT THE AUTHOR

Jean-Claude Izzo was born in Marseilles in 1945. Best known for the Marseilles trilogy (*Total Chaos*, *Chourmo*, *Solea*), Izzo is also the author of *The Lost Sailors*, and *A Sun for the Dying*. Izzo is widely credited with being the founder of the modern Mediterranean noir movement. He died in 2000 at the age of fifty-five.

www.europaeditions.com

EUROPA EDITIONS BACKLIST
(alphabetical by author)

Fiction

Carmine Abate
Between Two Seas • 978-1-933372-40-2 • Territories: World
The Homecoming Party • 978-1-933372-83-9 • Territories: World

Milena Agus
From the Land of the Moon • 978-1-60945-001-4 • Ebook • Territories:
World (excl. ANZ)

Salwa Al Neimi
The Proof of the Honey • 978-1-933372-68-6 • Ebook • Territories: World
(excl UK)

Simonetta Agnello Hornby
The Nun • 978-1-60945-062-5 • Territories: World

Daniel Arsand
Lovers • 978-1-60945-071-7 • Ebook • Territories: World

Jenn Ashworth
A Kind of Intimacy • 978-1-933372-86-0 • Territories: US & Can

Beryl Bainbridge
The Girl in the Polka Dot Dress • 978-1-60945-056-4 • Ebook •
Territories: US

Muriel Barbery
The Elegance of the Hedgehog • 978-1-933372-60-0 • Ebook • Territories:
World (excl. UK & EU)
Gourmet Rhapsody • 978-1-933372-95-2 • Ebook • Territories: World
(excl. UK & EU)

www.europaeditions.com

Stefano Benni
Margherita Dolce Vita • 978-1-933372-20-4 • Territories: World
Timeskipper • 978-1-933372-44-0 • Territories: World

Romano Bilenchi
The Chill • 978-1-933372-90-7 • Territories: World

Kazimierz Brandys
Rondo • 978-1-60945-004-5 • Territories: World

Alina Bronsky
Broken Glass Park • 978-1-933372-96-9 • Ebook • Territories: World
The Hottest Dishes of the Tartar Cuisine • 978-1-60945-006-9 • Ebook •
Territories: World

Jesse Browner
Everything Happens Today • 978-1-60945-051-9 • Ebook • Territories:
World (excl. UK & EU)

Francisco Coloane
Tierra del Fuego • 978-1-933372-63-1 • Ebook • Territories: World

Rebecca Connell
The Art of Losing • 978-1-933372-78-5 • Territories: US

Laurence Cossé
A Novel Bookstore • 978-1-933372-82-2 • Ebook • Territories: World
An Accident in August • 978-1-60945-049-6 • Territories: World (excl. UK)

Diego De Silva
I Hadn't Understood • 978-1-60945-065-6 • Territories: World

Shashi Deshpande
The Dark Holds No Terrors • 978-1-933372-67-9 • Territories: US

www.europaeditions.com

Steve Erickson
Zeroville • 978-1-933372-39-6 • Territories: US & Can
These Dreams of You • 978-1-60945-063-2 • Territories: US & Can

Elena Ferrante
The Days of Abandonment • 978-1-933372-00-6 • Ebook • Territories: World
Troubling Love • 978-1-933372-16-7 • Territories: World
The Lost Daughter • 978-1-933372-42-6 • Territories: World

Linda Ferri
Cecilia • 978-1-933372-87-7 • Territories: World

Damon Galgut
In a Strange Room • 978-1-60945-011-3 • Ebook • Territories: USA

Santiago Gamboa
Necropolis • 978-1-60945-073-1 • Ebook • Territories: World

Jane Gardam
Old Filth • 978-1-933372-13-6 • Ebook • Territories: US
The Queen of the Tambourine • 978-1-933372-36-5 • Ebook • Territories: US
The People on Privilege Hill • 978-1-933372-56-3 • Ebook • Territories: US
The Man in the Wooden Hat • 978-1-933372-89-1 • Ebook • Territories: US
God on the Rocks • 978-1-933372-76-1 • Ebook • Territories: US
Crusoe's Daughter • 978-1-60945-069-4 • Ebook • Territories: US

Anna Gavalda
French Leave • 978-1-60945-005-2 • Ebook • Territories: US & Can

Seth Greenland
The Angry Buddhist • 978-1-60945-068-7 • Ebook • Territories: World

Katharina Hacker
The Have-Nots • 978-1-933372-41-9 • Territories: World (excl. India)

www.europaeditions.com

Patrick Hamilton
Hangover Square • 978-1-933372-06-8 • Territories: US & Can

James Hamilton-Paterson
Cooking with Fernet Branca • 978-1-933372-01-3 • Territories: US
Amazing Disgrace • 978-1-933372-19-8 • Territories: US
Rancid Pansies • 978-1-933372-62-4 • Territories: USA

Alfred Hayes
The Girl on the Via Flaminia • 978-1-933372-24-2 • Ebook •
Territories: World

Jean-Claude Izzo
The Lost Sailors • 978-1-933372-35-8 • Territories: World
A Sun for the Dying • 978-1-933372-59-4 • Territories: World

Gail Jones
Sorry • 978-1-933372-55-6 • Territories: US & Can

Ioanna Karystiani
The Jasmine Isle • 978-1-933372-10-5 • Territories: World
Swell • 978-1-933372-98-3 • Territories: World

Peter Kocan
Fresh Fields • 978-1-933372-29-7 • Territories: US, EU & Can
The Treatment and the Cure • 978-1-933372-45-7 • Territories: US, EU & Can

Helmut Krausser
Eros • 978-1-933372-58-7 • Territories: World

Amara Lakhous
Clash of Civilizations Over an Elevator in Piazza Vittorio •
978-1-933372-61-7 • Ebook • Territories: World
Divorce Islamic Style • 978-1-60945-066-3 • Ebook • Territories: World

www.europaeditions.com

Lia Levi
The Jewish Husband • 978-1-933372-93-8 • Territories: World

Valerio Massimo Manfredi
The Ides of March • 978-1-933372-99-0 • Territories: US

Leïla Marouane
The Sexual Life of an Islamist in Paris • 978-1-933372-85-3 •
Territories: World

Lorenzo Mediano
The Frost on His Shoulders • 978-1-60945-072-4 • Ebook •
Territories: World

Sélim Nassib
I Loved You for Your Voice • 978-1-933372-07-5 • Territories: World
The Palestinian Lover • 978-1-933372-23-5 • Territories: World

Amélie Nothomb
Tokyo Fiancée • 978-1-933372-64-8 • Territories: US & Can
Hygiene and the Assassin • 978-1-933372-77-8 • Ebook • Territories: US & Can

Valeria Parrella
For Grace Received • 978-1-933372-94-5 • Territories: World

Alessandro Piperno
The Worst Intentions • 978-1-933372-33-4 • Territories: World
Persecution • 978-1-60945-074-8 • Ebook • Territories: World

Lorcan Roche
The Companion • 978-1-933372-84-6 • Territories: World

Boualem Sansal
The German Mujahid • 978-1-933372-92-1 • Ebook • Territories: US & Can

www.europaeditions.com

Eric-Emmanuel Schmitt
The Most Beautiful Book in the World • 978-1-933372-74-7 • Ebook •
Territories: World
The Woman with the Bouquet • 978-1-933372-81-5 • Ebook • Territories:
US & Can

Angelika Schrobsdorff
You Are Not Like Other Mothers • 978-1-60945-075-5 • Ebook •
Territories: World

Audrey Schulman
Three Weeks in December • 978-1-60945-064-9 • Ebook • Territories: US
& Can

James Scudamore
Heliopolis • 978-1-933372-73-0 • Ebook • Territories: US

Luis Sepúlveda
The Shadow of What We Were • 978-1-60945-002-1 • Ebook • Territories:
World

Paolo Sorrentino
Everybody's Right • 978-1-60945-052-6 • Ebook • Territories: US & Can

Domenico Starnone
First Execution • 978-1-933372-66-2 • Territories: World

Henry Sutton
Get Me out of Here • 978-1-60945-007-6 • Ebook • Territories: US & Can

Chad Taylor
Departure Lounge • 978-1-933372-09-9 • Territories: US, EU & Can

www.europaeditions.com

Roma Tearne
Mosquito • 978-1-933372-57-0 • Territories: US & Can
Bone China • 978-1-933372-75-4 • Territories: US

André Carl van der Merwe
Moffie • 978-1-60945-050-2 • Ebook • Territories: World
(excl. S. Africa)

Fay Weldon
Chalcot Crescent • 978-1-933372-79-2 • Territories: US

Anne Wiazemsky
My Berlin Child • 978-1-60945-003-8 • Territories: US & Can

Jonathan Yardley
Second Reading • 978-1-60945-008-3 • Ebook • Territories: US & Can

Edwin M. Yoder Jr.
Lions at Lamb House • 978-1-933372-34-1 • Territories: World

Michele Zackheim
Broken Colors • 978-1-933372-37-2 • Territories: World

Alice Zeniter
Take This Man • 978-1-60945-053-3 • Territories: World

Tonga Books

Ian Holding
Of Beasts and Beings • 978-1-60945-054-0 • Ebook • Territories: US & Can

Sara Levine
Treasure Island!!! • 978-0-14043-768-3 • Ebook • Territories: World

www.europaeditions.com

Alexander Maksik
You Deserve Nothing • 978-1-60945-048-9 • Ebook • Territories: US, Can
& EU (excl. UK)

Thad Ziolkowski
Wichita • 978-1-60945-070-0 • Ebook • Territories: World

Crime/Noir

Massimo Carlotto
The Goodbye Kiss • 978-1-933372-05-1 • Ebook • Territories: World
Death's Dark Abyss • 978-1-933372-18-1 • Ebook • Territories: World
The Fugitive • 978-1-933372-25-9 • Ebook • Territories: World
Bandit Love • 978-1-933372-80-8 • Ebook • Territories: World
Poisonville • 978-1-933372-91-4 • Ebook • Territories: World

Giancarlo De Cataldo
The Father and the Foreigner • 978-1-933372-72-3 • Territories: World

Caryl Férey
Zulu • 978-1-933372-88-4 • Ebook • Territories: World (excl. UK & EU)
Utu • 978-1-60945-055-7 • Ebook • Territories: World (excl. UK & EU)

Alicia Giménez-Bartlett
Dog Day • 978-1-933372-14-3 • Territories: US & Can
Prime Time Suspect • 978-1-933372-31-0 • Territories: US & Can
Death Rites • 978-1-933372-54-9 • Territories: US & Can

Jean-Claude Izzo
Total Chaos • 978-1-933372-04-4 • Territories: US & Can
Chourmo • 978-1-933372-17-4 • Territories: US & Can
Solea • 978-1-933372-30-3 • Territories: US & Can

www.europaeditions.com

Matthew F. Jones
Boot Tracks • 978-1-933372-11-2 • Territories: US & Can

Gene Kerrigan
The Midnight Choir • 978-1-933372-26-6 • Territories: US & Can
Little Criminals • 978-1-933372-43-3 • Territories: US & Can

Carlo Lucarelli
Carte Blanche • 978-1-933372-15-0 • Territories: World
The Damned Season • 978-1-933372-27-3 • Territories: World
Via delle Oche • 978-1-933372-53-2 • Territories: World

Edna Mazya
Love Burns • 978-1-933372-08-2 • Territories: World (excl. ANZ)

Yishai Sarid
Limassol • 978-1-60945-000-7 • Ebook • Territories: World (excl. UK, AUS & India)

Joel Stone
The Jerusalem File • 978-1-933372-65-5 • Ebook • Territories: World

Benjamin Tammuz
Minotaur • 978-1-933372-02-0 • Ebook • Territories: World

Non-fiction

Alberto Angela
A Day in the Life of Ancient Rome • 978-1-933372-71-6 • Territories: World • History

www.europaeditions.com

Helmut Dubiel
Deep In the Brain: Living with Parkinson's Disease • 978-1-933372-70-9 •
Ebook • Territories: World • Medicine/Memoir

James Hamilton-Paterson
Seven-Tenths: The Sea and Its Thresholds • 978-1-933372-69-3 • Territories:
USA • Nature/Essays

Daniele Mastrogiacomo
Days of Fear • 978-1-933372-97-6 • Ebook • Territories: World • Current
affairs/Memoir/Afghanistan/Journalism

Valery Panyushkin
Twelve Who Don't Agree • 978-1-60945-010-6 • Ebook • Territories:
World • Current affairs/Memoir/Russia/Journalism

Christa Wolf
One Day a Year: 1960-2000 • 978-1-933372-22-8 • Territories: World •
Memoir/History/20th Century

Children's Illustrated Fiction

Altan
Here Comes Timpa • 978-1-933372-28-0 • Territories: World (excl. Italy)
Timpa Goes to the Sea • 978-1-933372-32-7 • Territories: World (excl. Italy)
Fairy Tale Timpa • 978-1-933372-38-9 • Territories: World (excl. Italy)

'f Erlbruch
'g Question • 978-1-933372-03-7 • Territories: US & Can
'cle of the Bears • 978-1-933372-21-1 • Territories: US & Can
onda Belli) The Butterfly Workshop • 978-1-933372-12-9 •
'S & Can